AF593967

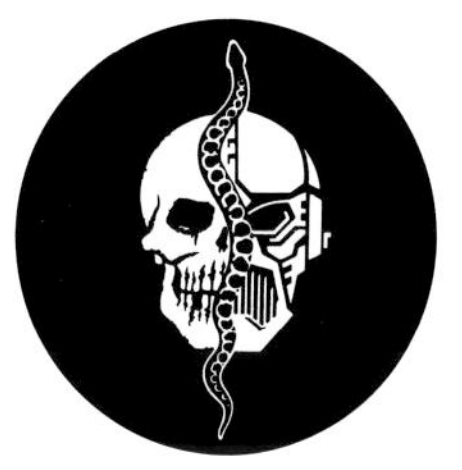

LUIS ROYO

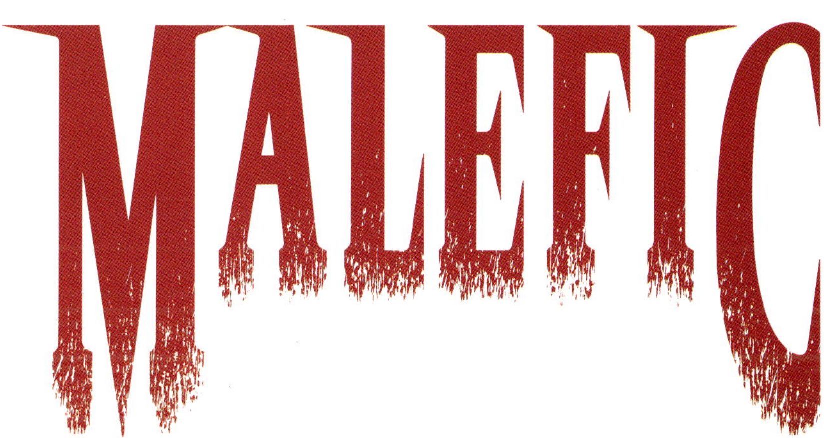

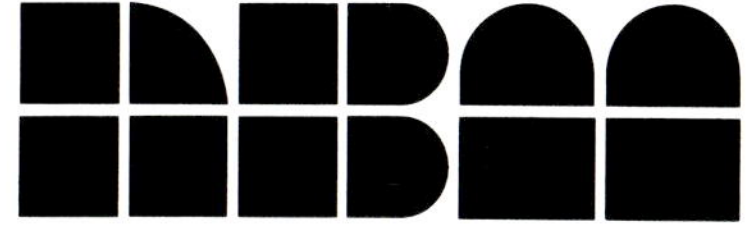

ISBN 1-56163-181-7

Translation by Robert Legault
Printed in Spain

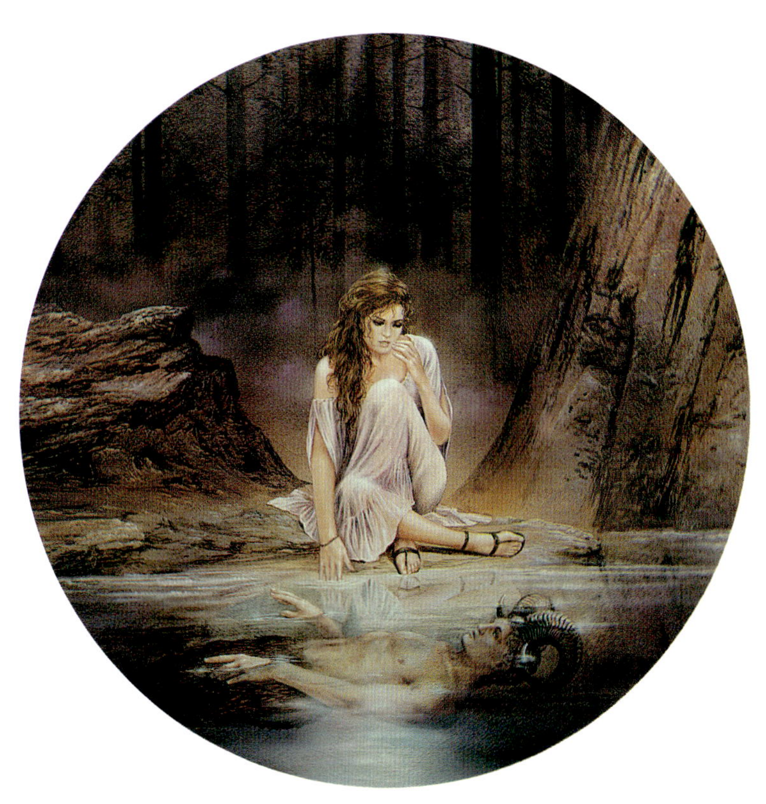

LANDSCAPES WITH FIGURES

There are works of art that seduce me by their very presence. Others provoke me; they awaken something inside me that I would rather let sleep. I guess it must happen to everybody.

Luis Royo, with an alchemist's patience and an obsessive thoroughness, makes images that bring out that same reaction of mystification and uneasiness. It's useless to try to figure out the hidden clues, the cook's secrets, the whys and wherefores. Beyond that, there's an uncontrollable vertigo that makes a mockery of theories and rationalizations.

Luis deliberately perverts whatever he paints. There are sure to be people who don't realize this, who just see his images as a woman with a fantastic background. With a malevolent mastery, Luis works through a classic sort of painting (the landscape with figure) and uses a classic theme (the eternal myth of Beauty and the Beast) --but he turns it around, giving us beauties who are cold and distant, with a look of feline indifference; self-sufficient and yet incongruously attractive in the midst of his gloomy settings. These women are the counterpoint to these sober compositions.

He fills his airbrush with darkness and spreads it left and right with virtuous accuracy. He paints thick, Lovecraftian fogs, the kind that wrap everything in gloom, like vapors from cheesy special effects. He undergoes the penance (or the exorcism) of painting the thousand cracks of an eroded stone, the folds of the skins of mythical animals, the reflections on the surfaces of magic ponds, the sparkle of forgotten metals, the different colors of the bones of some unknown being...and manages to make all of them look unnatural and thus disturbing.

This pile of paradoxes, of wrong appearances, of perverse connections with the collective unconscious, is what disarms the more attentive viewer of this disturbing panorama. The others, those who simply look at the surface, are perhaps just victims taken in by the high quality of draftsmanship that any realistic work of high quality has. And there are those who only want to remain complacently fascinated by the perfection of such images.

An illustrator sees his work disseminated in the covers and interiors of endless publications of all sorts. But it's difficult to get a complete vision of his work. Until now. Enter the maelstrom.

Miguelanxo Prado

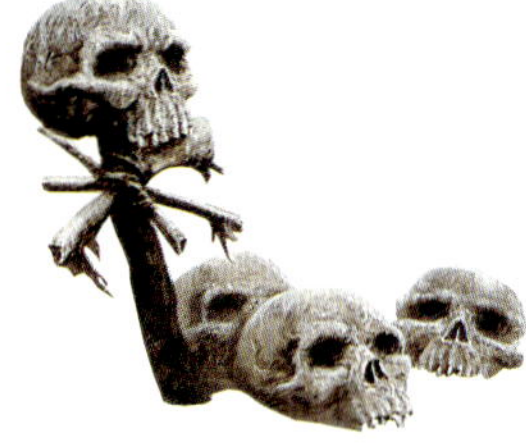

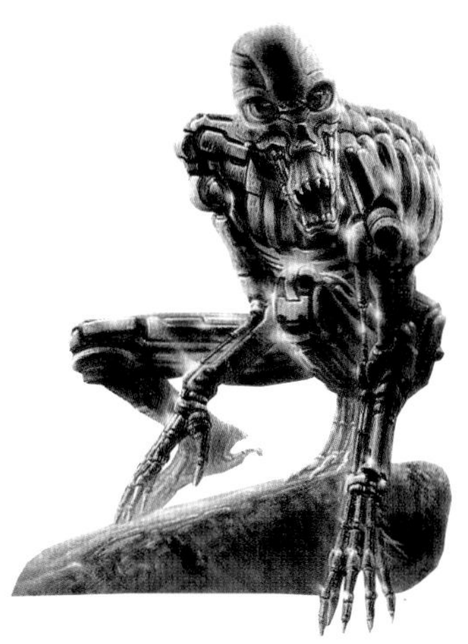

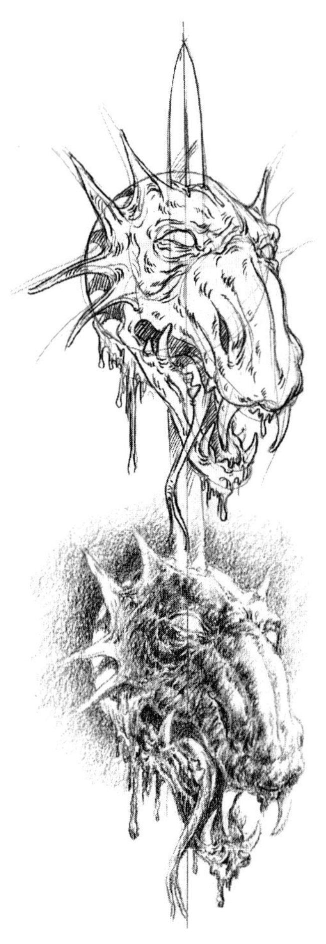

■ BIFID CHIAROSCURO
1993
Beneath the hardness of the night there is beauty. Sensuality is half hidden by cold metal. An image burns itself into our retinas--and the drama begins.

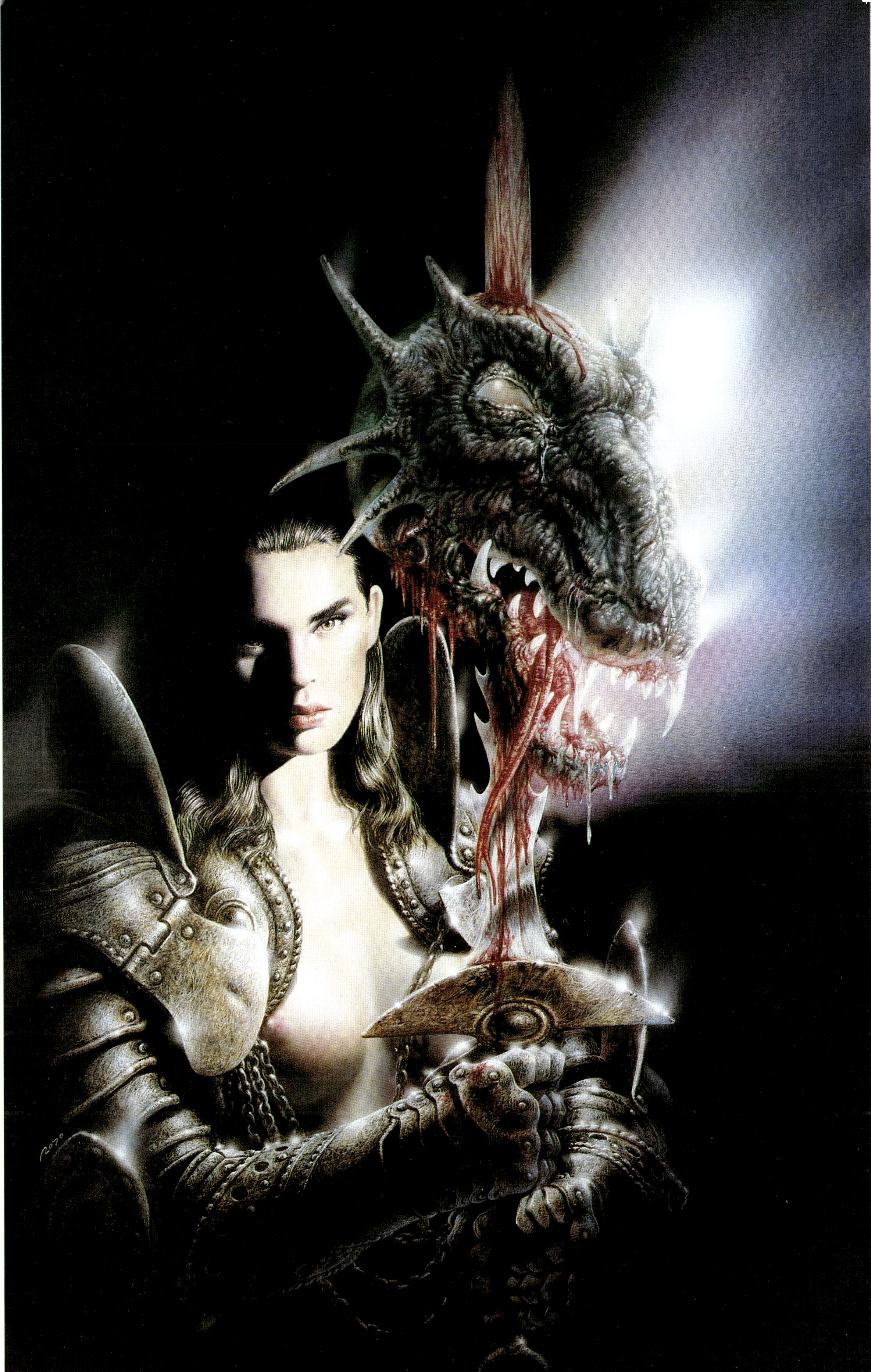

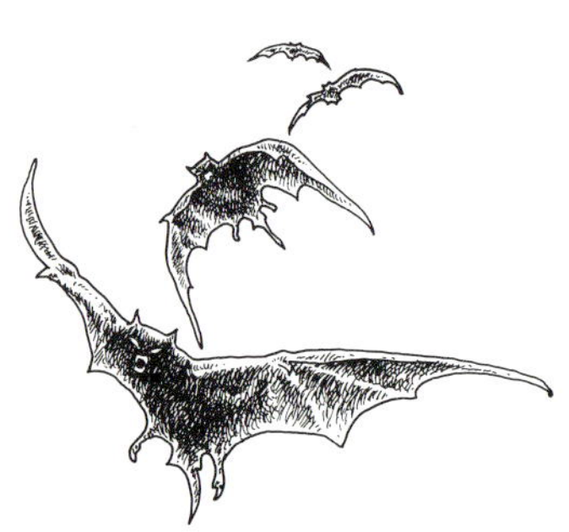

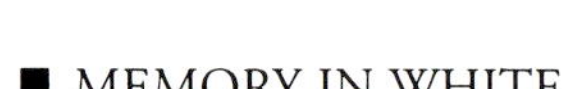

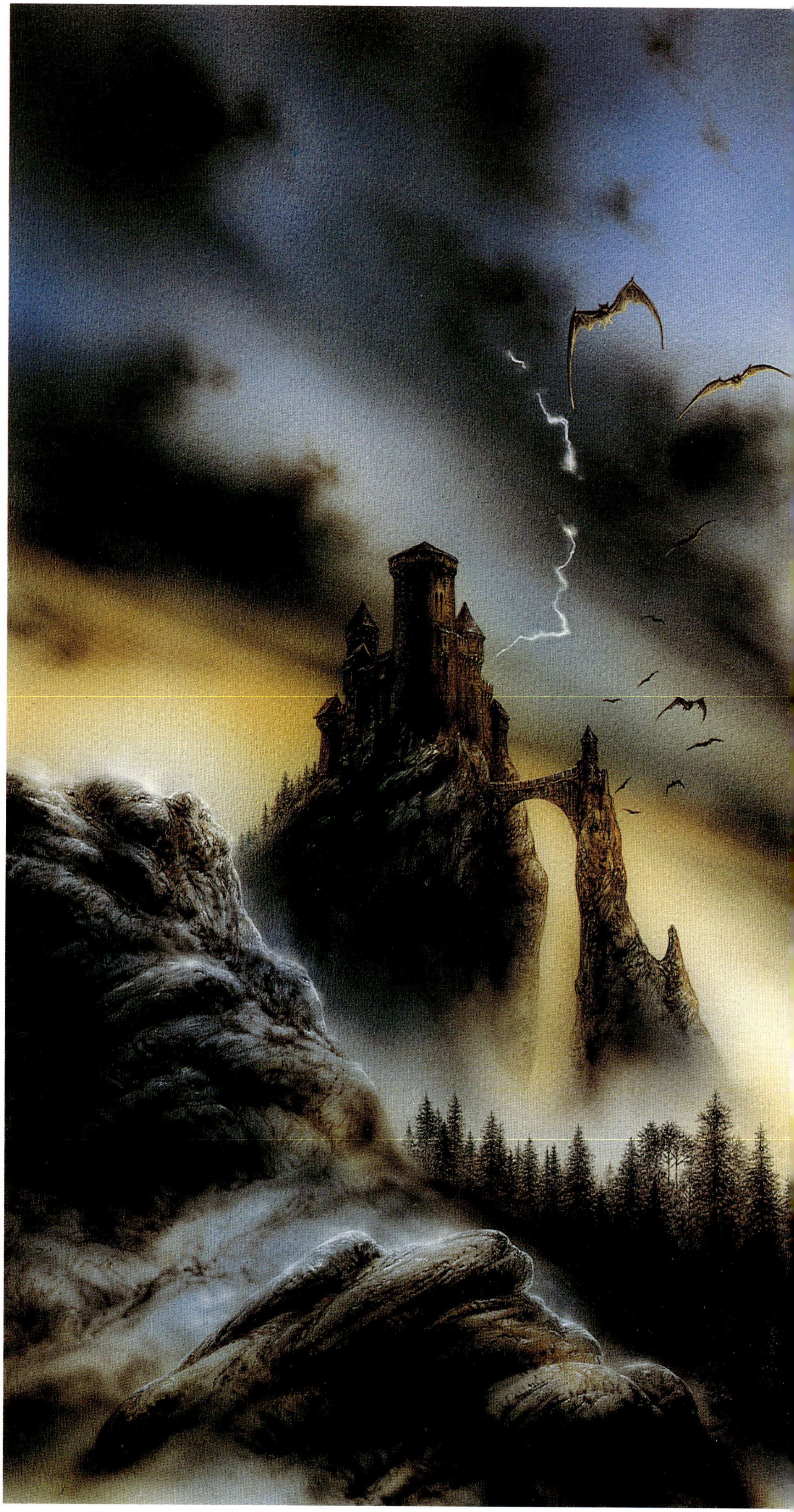

■ MEMORY IN WHITE
1993
Concentric circles lead us to childhood memories. When we raise the lid of the coffin where we buried the "I" we used to be, out come fairies, dragons, unicorns, elves, and castles.

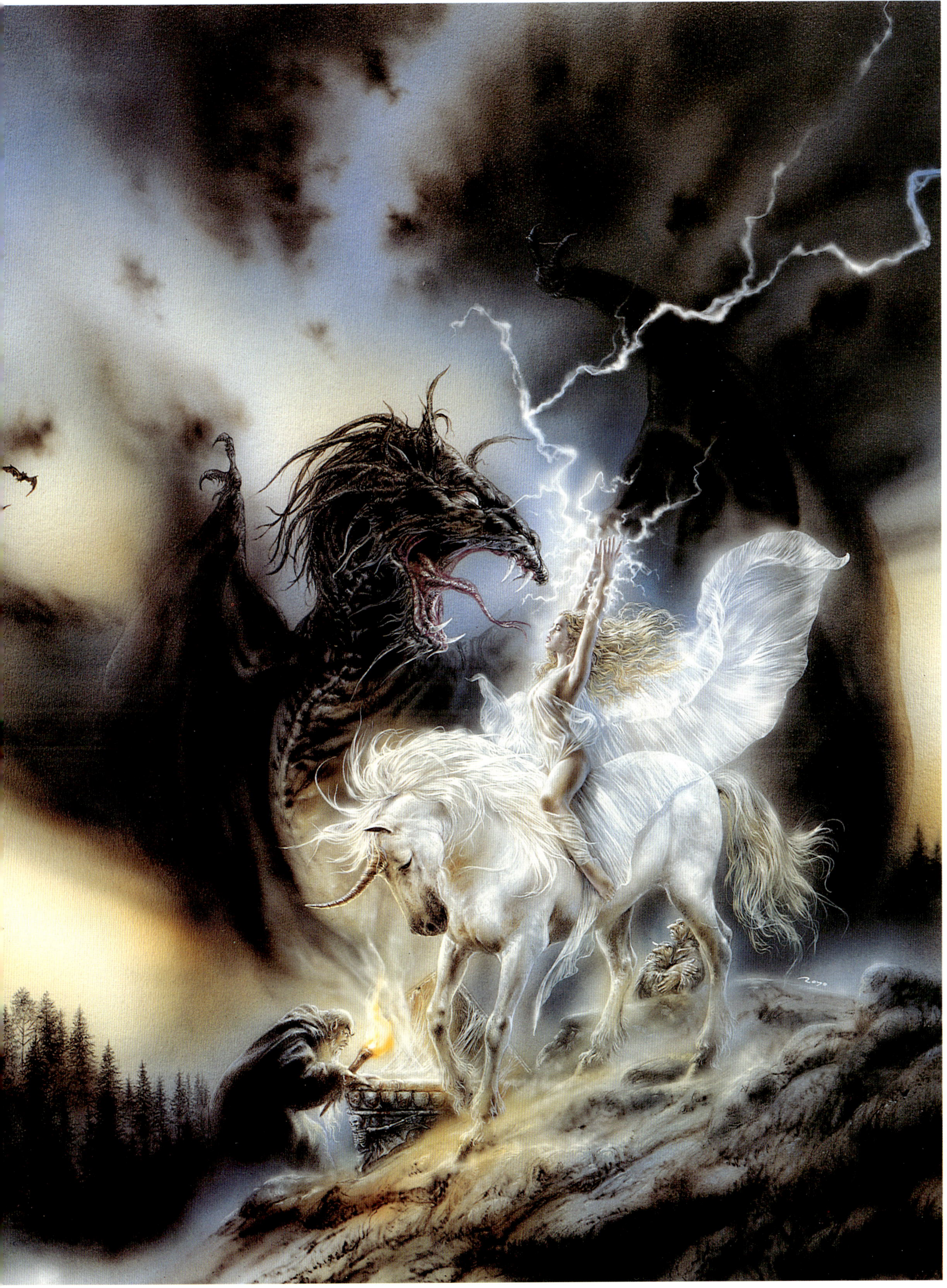

■ WINGS OF REFLECTION

1993

Reflections of images, where monstrous existence gets confused with ethereal dreams. A shining and desirable dream reflected together with the transfixed, humiliated skull of...reality?

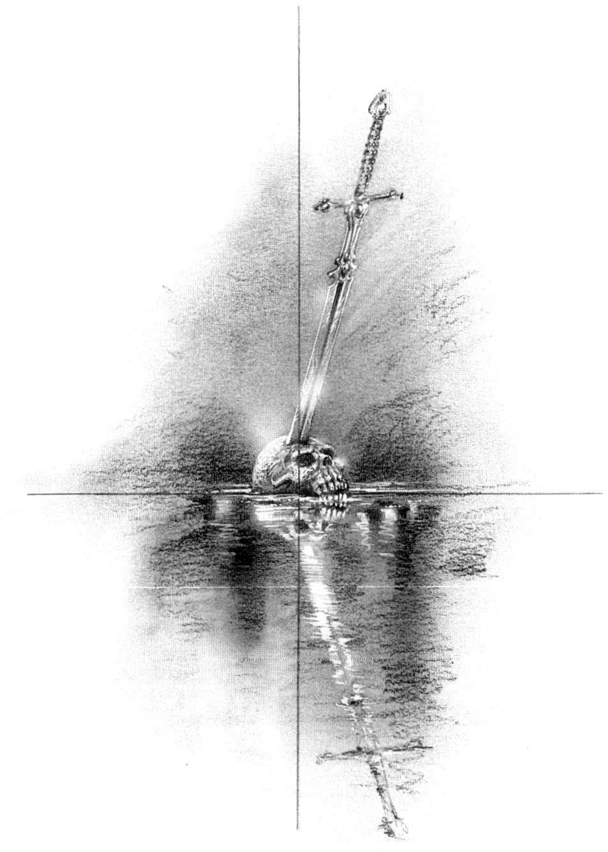

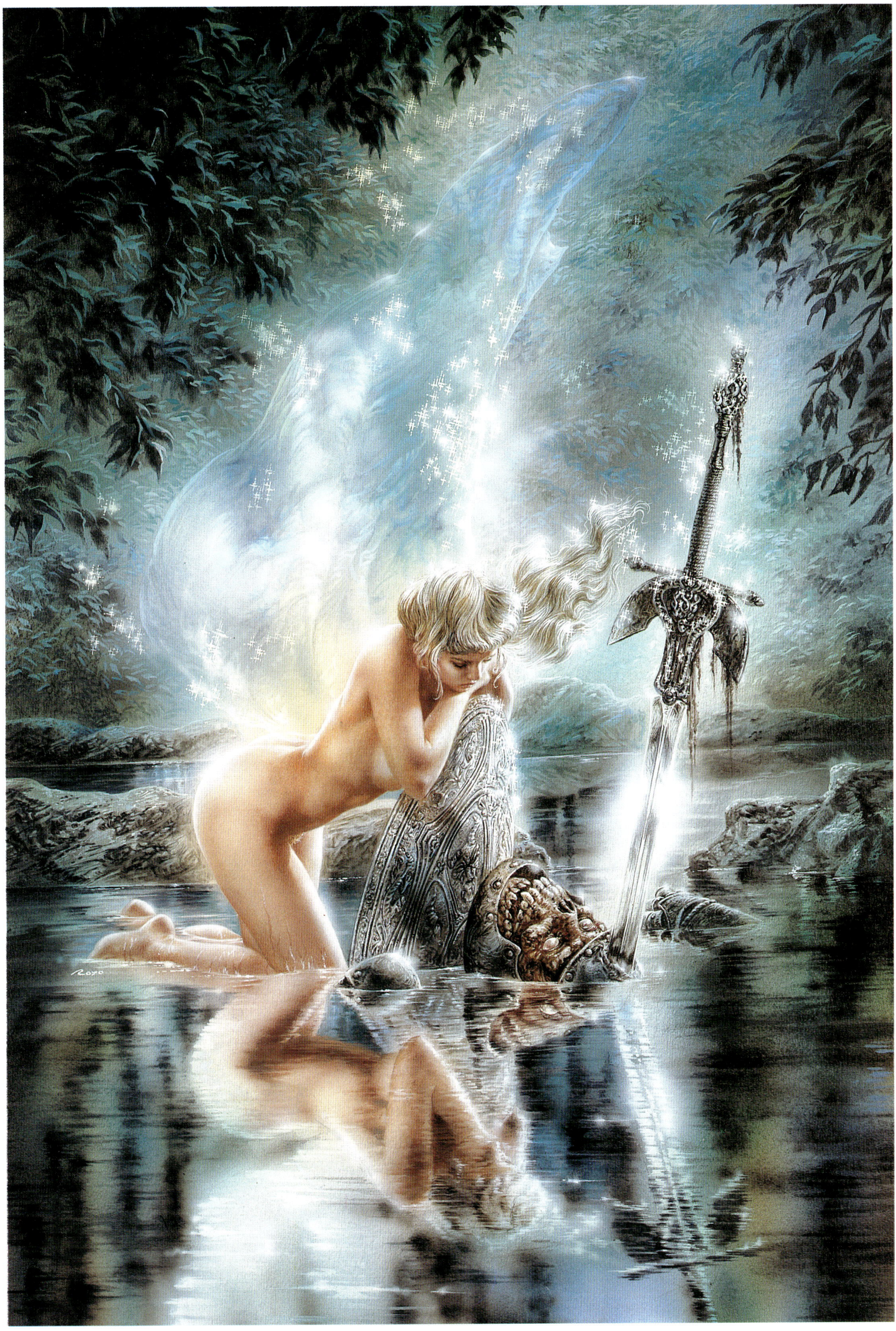
Royo

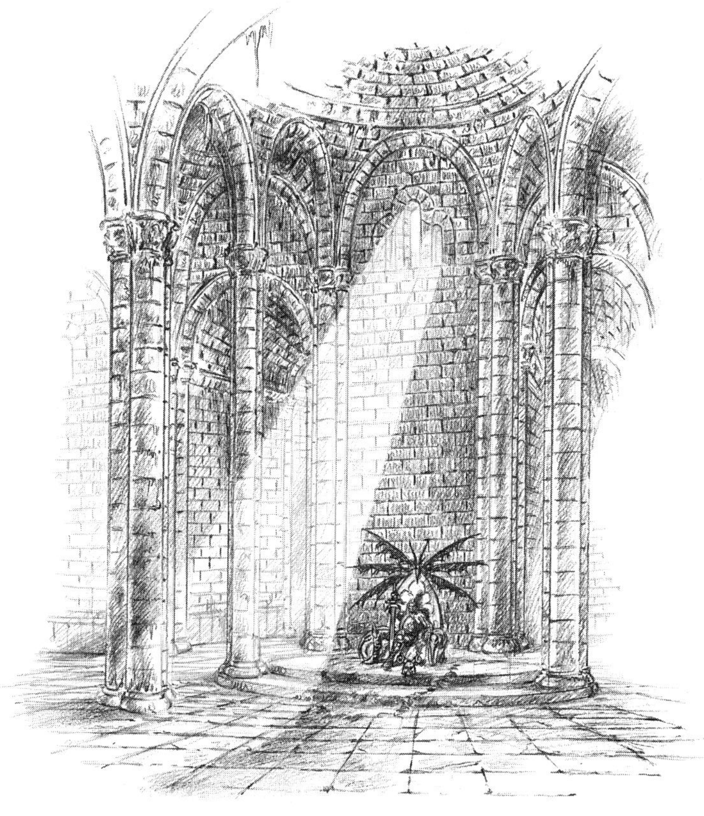

■ CORALLED BY SWEAT

1992

An eternal scene: the warrior in repose. A few dark drops reveal his hard past. An expression, like the salt of sweat, and his weariness reflected in the hand which once took up the sword.

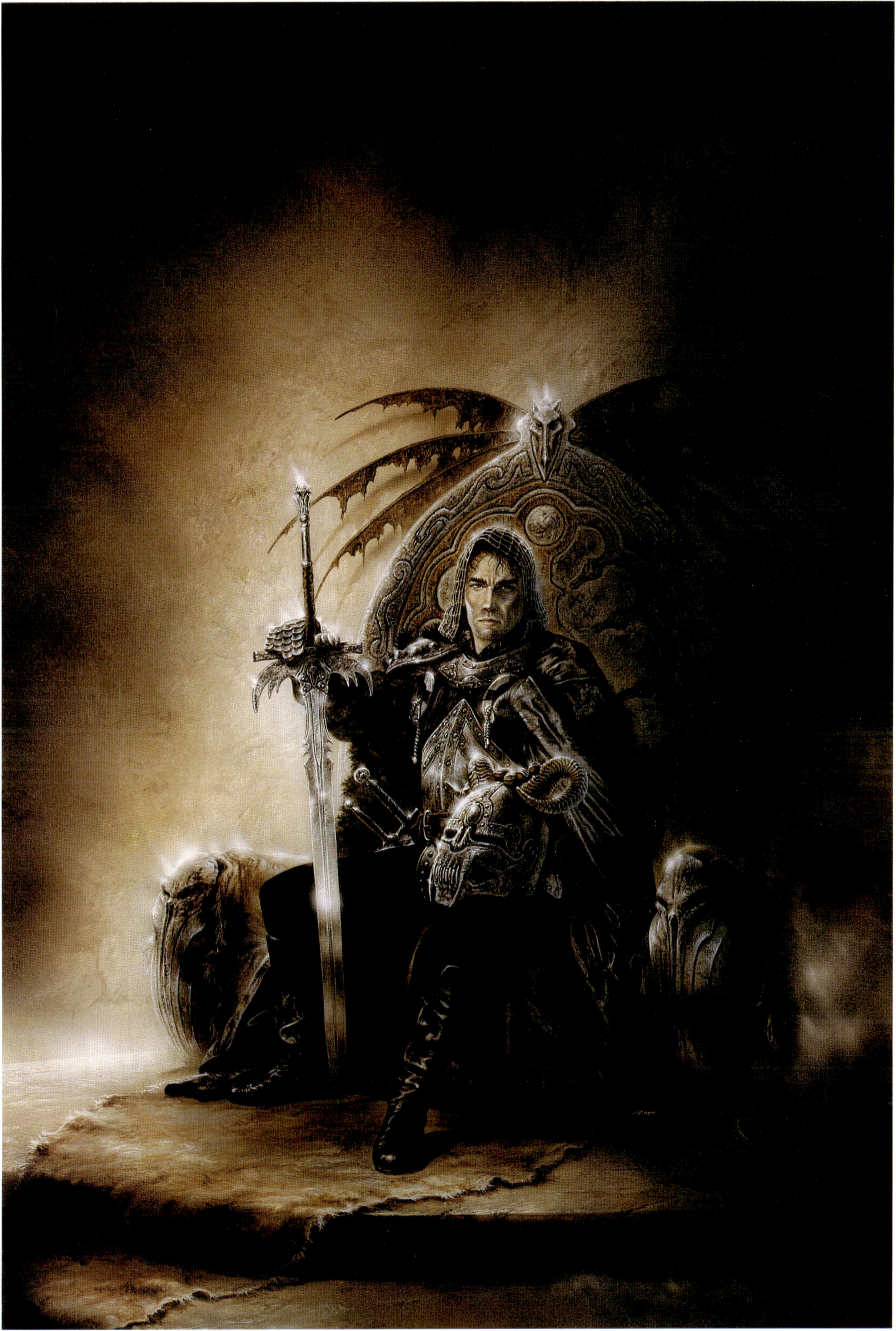

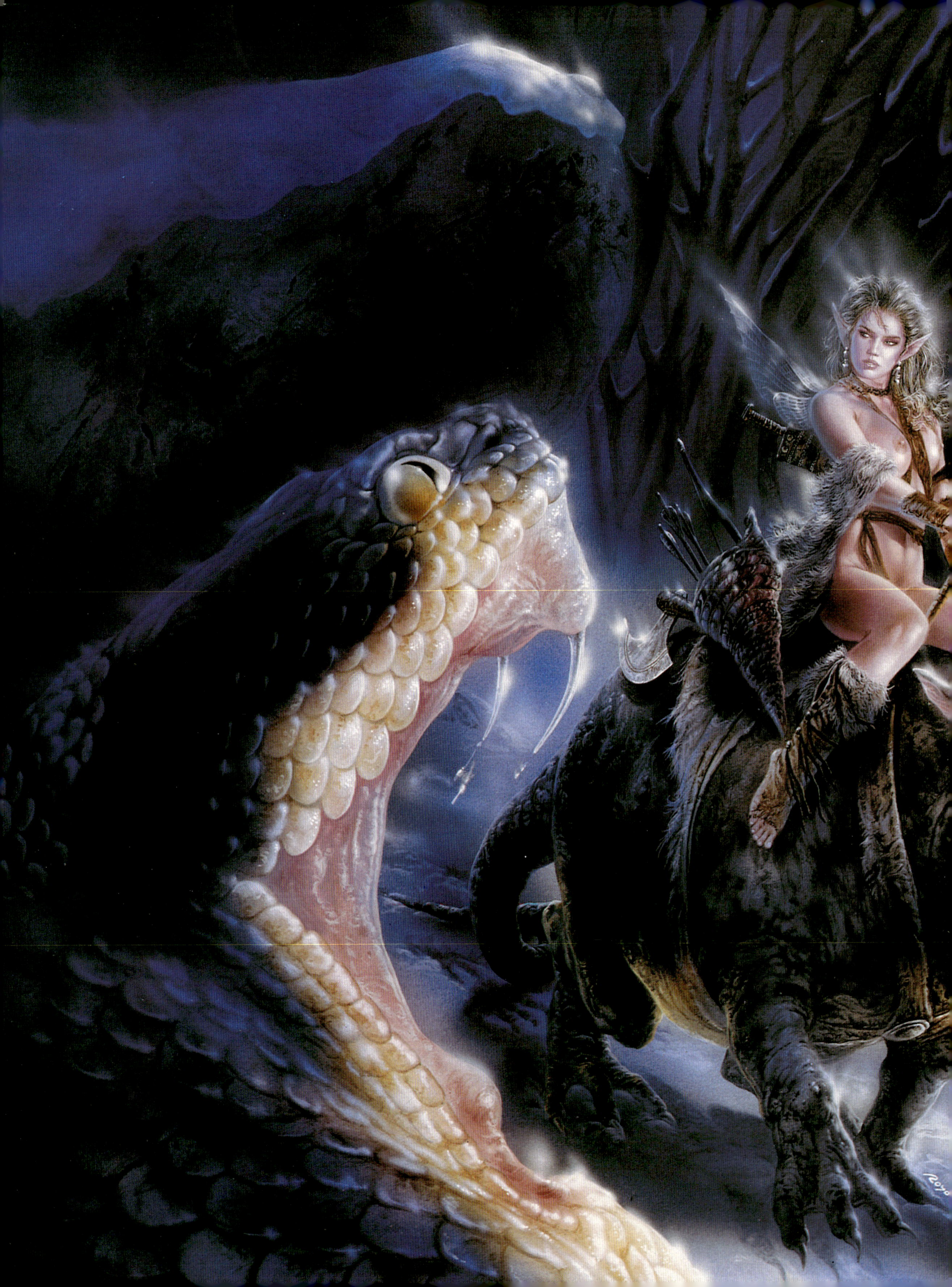

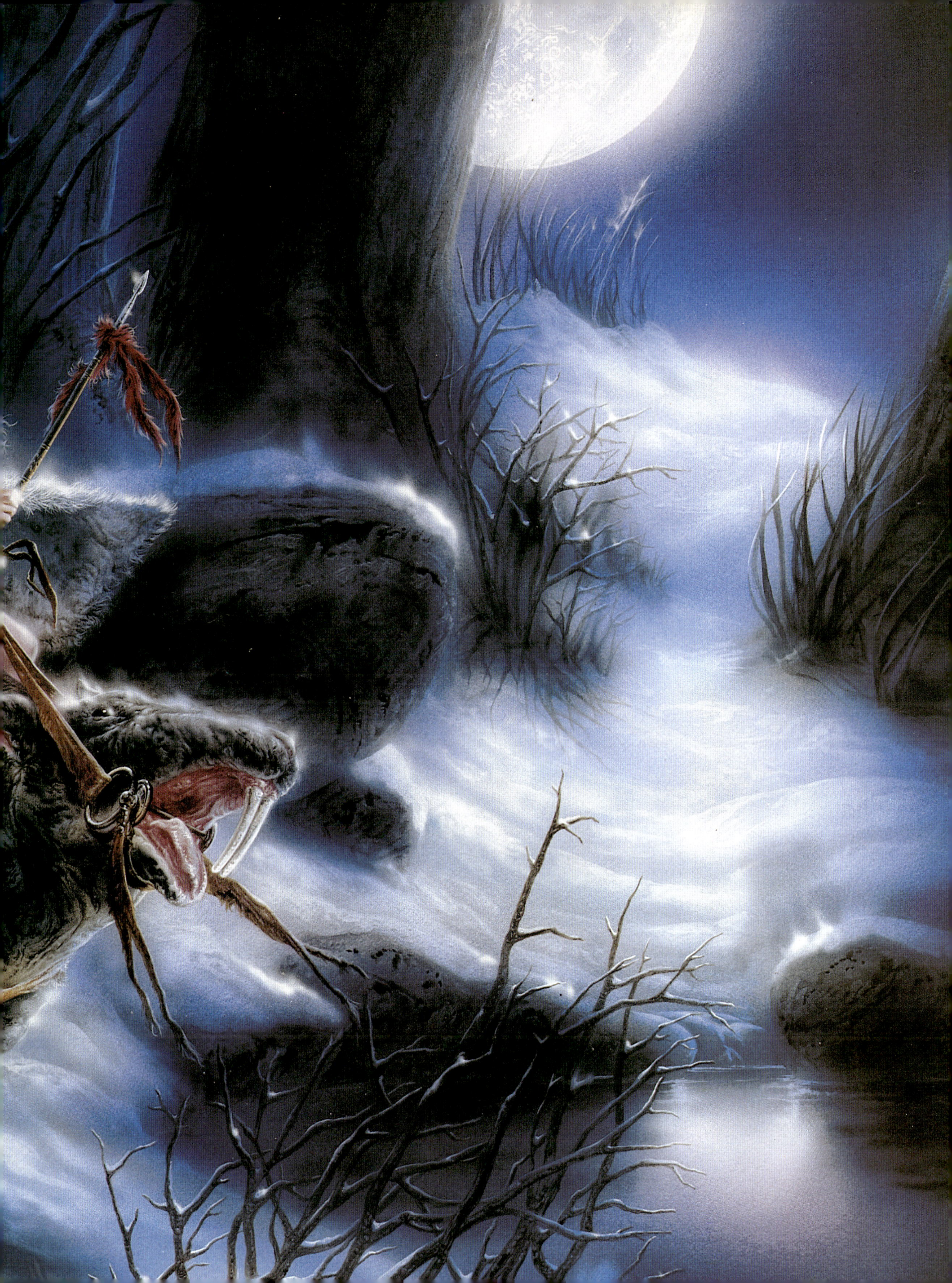

◄ WINGS OF A DREAM

1992

A tale of snowy days, of fairies and moons. A place where long ears don't mean breasts can't be voluptuous, where butterfly wings don't mean closed thighs, where moonlight doesn't obscure a sensuous expression, and where danger doesn't bring out fear, but defiance.

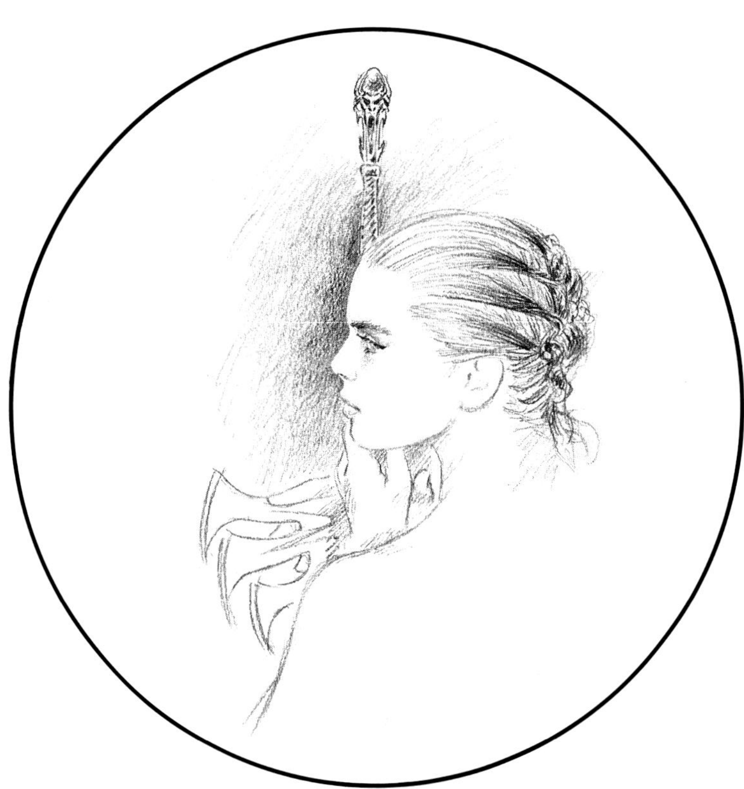

■ LIGHT OF PANIC

1994

Hung up for days by light.
Light of space to reflect dreams.
Light of beauty to see how small we are.
Light of a look to drown in.

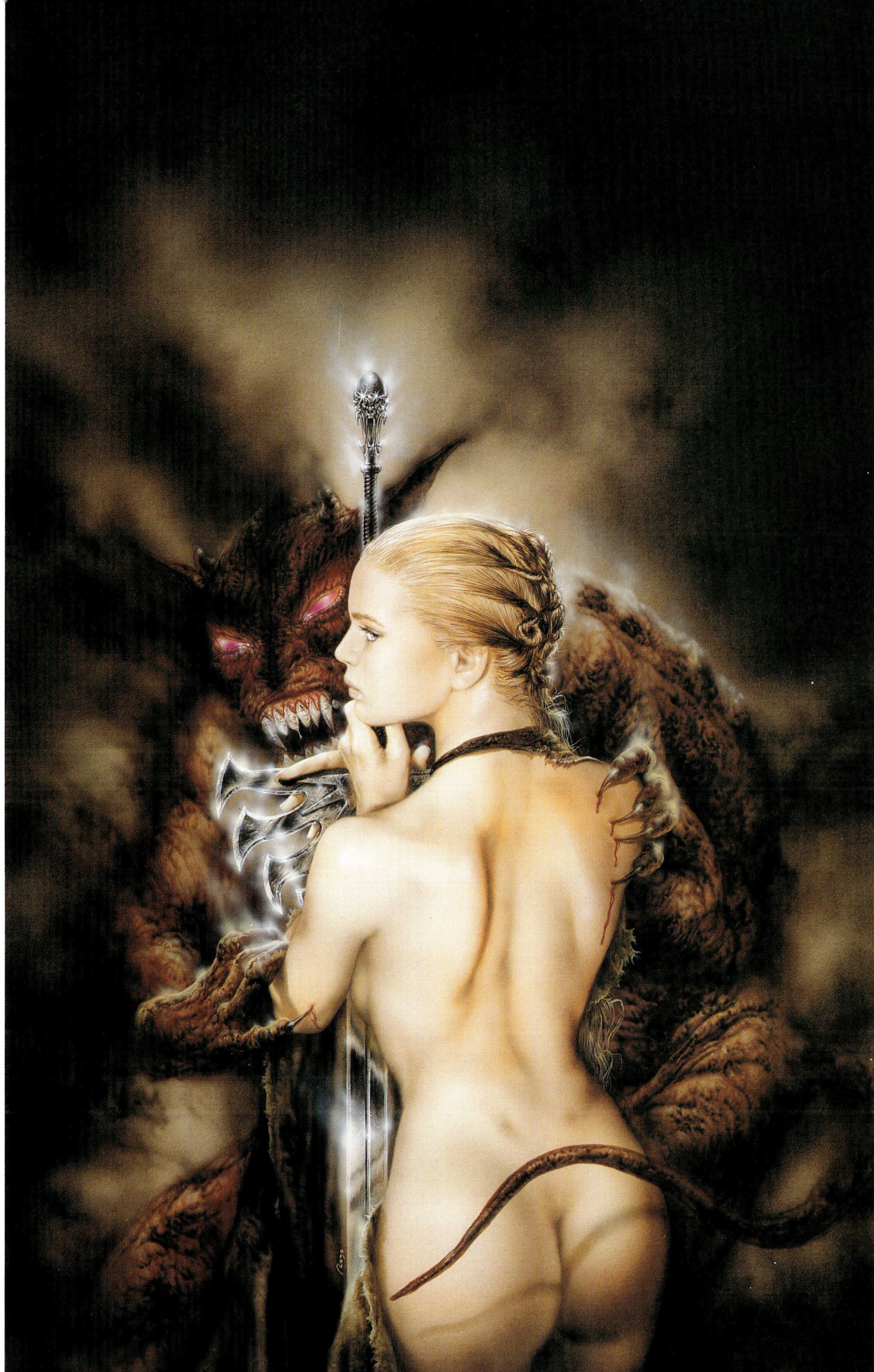

■ WINNER TAKES ALL

1990

When a work gets complicated due to the required information that a commission has to contain, it's good to fall back on geometry. Weapons, arms, legs, and even architecture can form perpendicular lines that multiply the subjects to infinity.

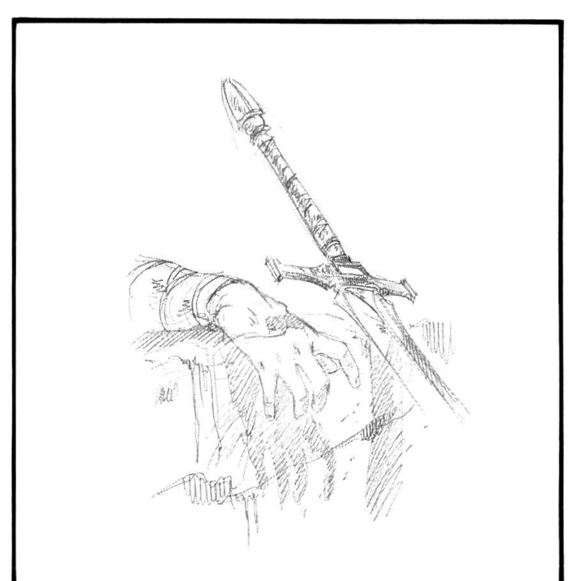

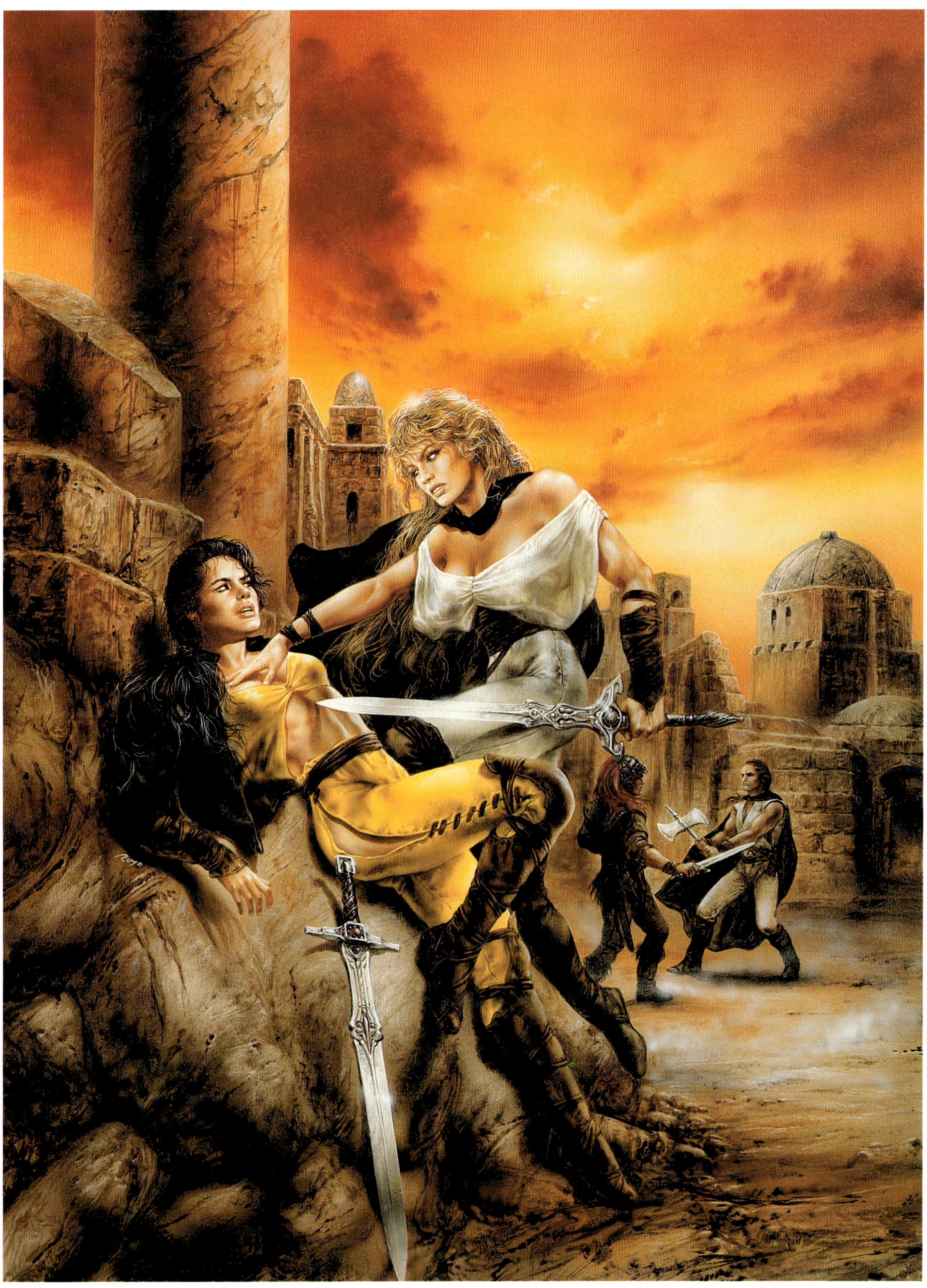

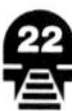

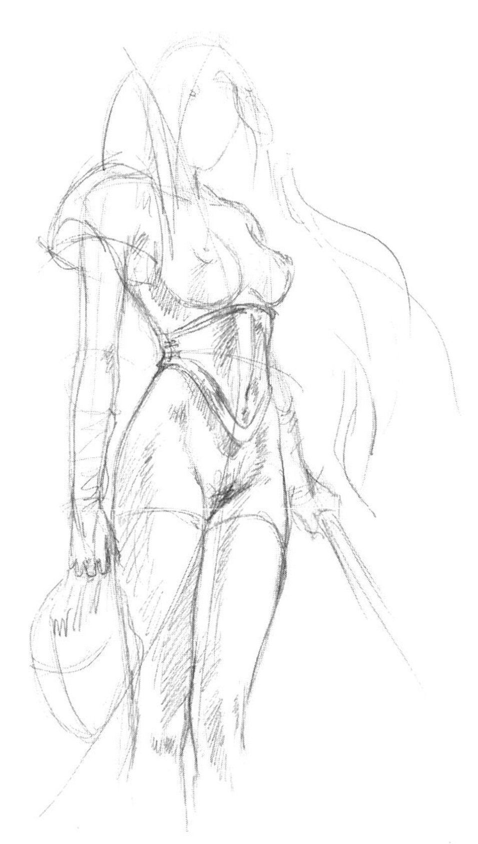

■ THE PENDULUM'S PAUSE

1993

Defining and polishing an image can work against its message, depriving us of the mood and the magic of its suggestions.

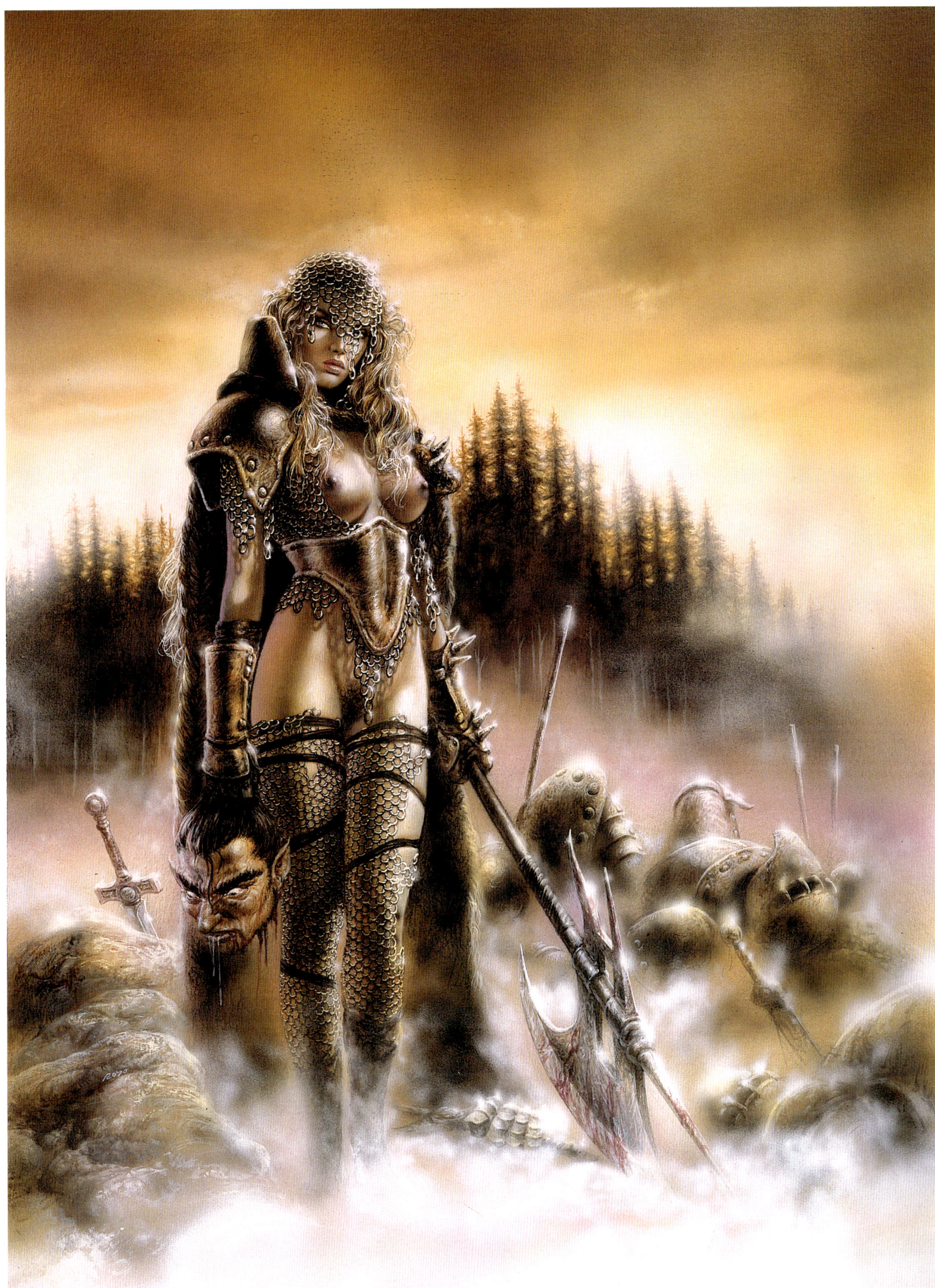

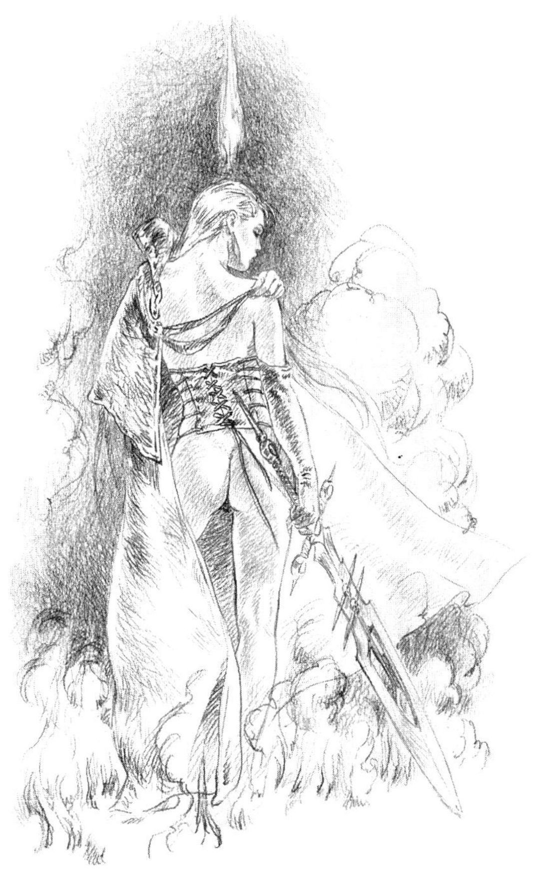

■ THE SEEDS OF NOTHING
1994
From the trips I now and then take to childhood, I brought back, for this illustration, a bag of old religious images, solitary desires, and nightmares.

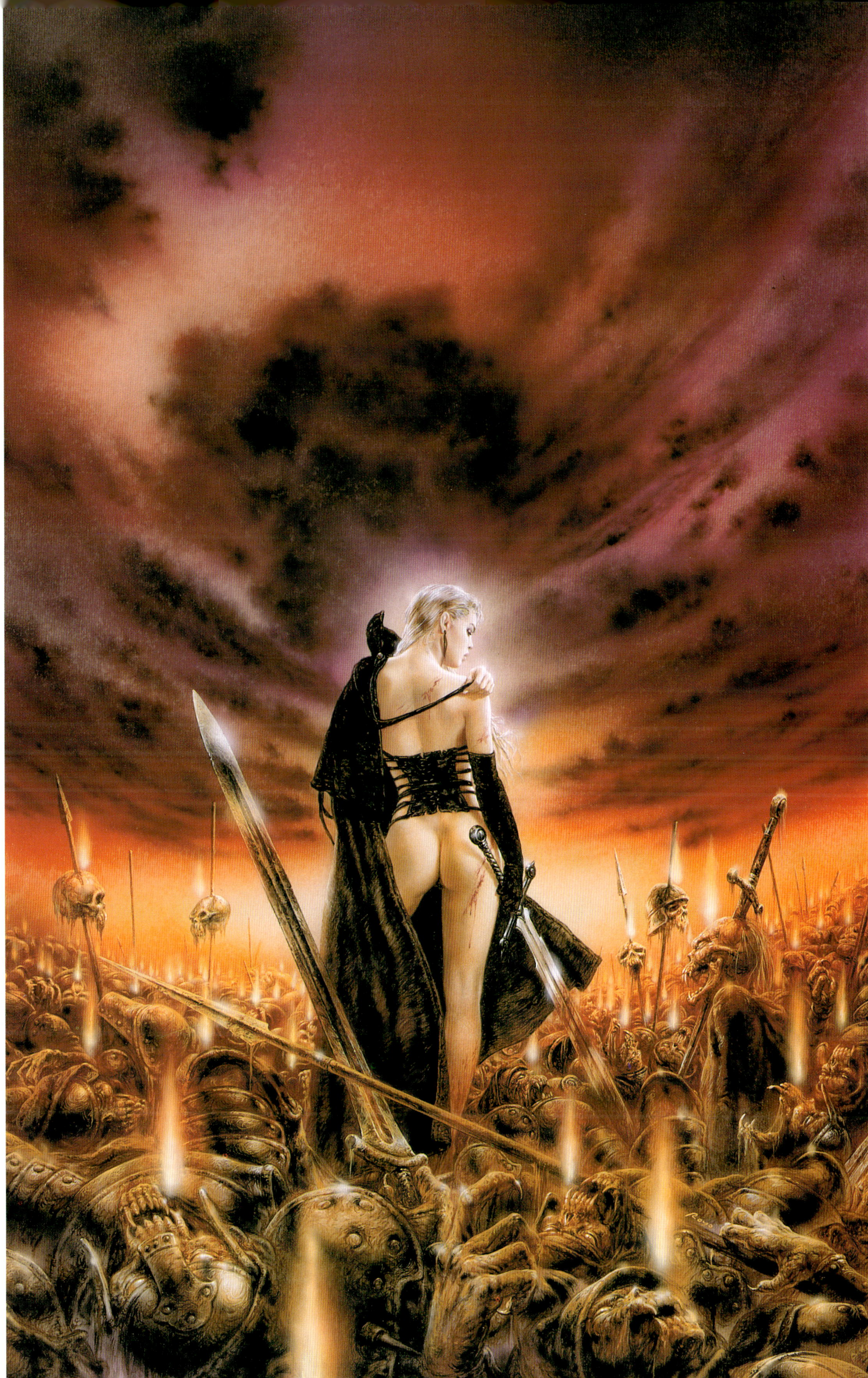

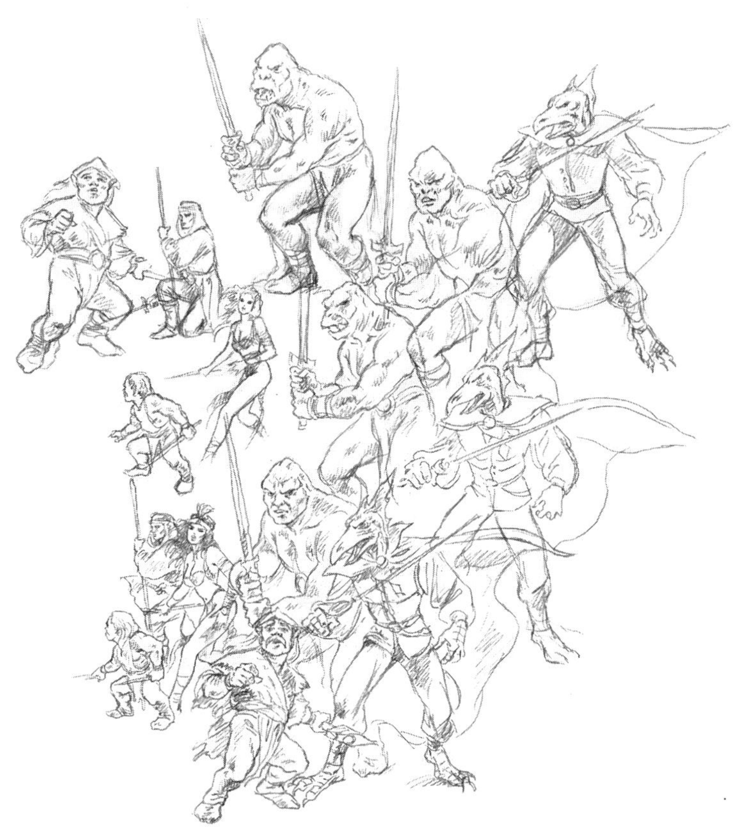

■ MISTS OF BETRAYAL

1993

Editorial instructions aren't always limitations for an artist; sometimes they help him keep a grip so he won't sink down into the darkness inside him and cry. Imaginary universes take you back to a place of adventure, of danger, and your friends take on a resemblance to faces lost in the attic of your mind.

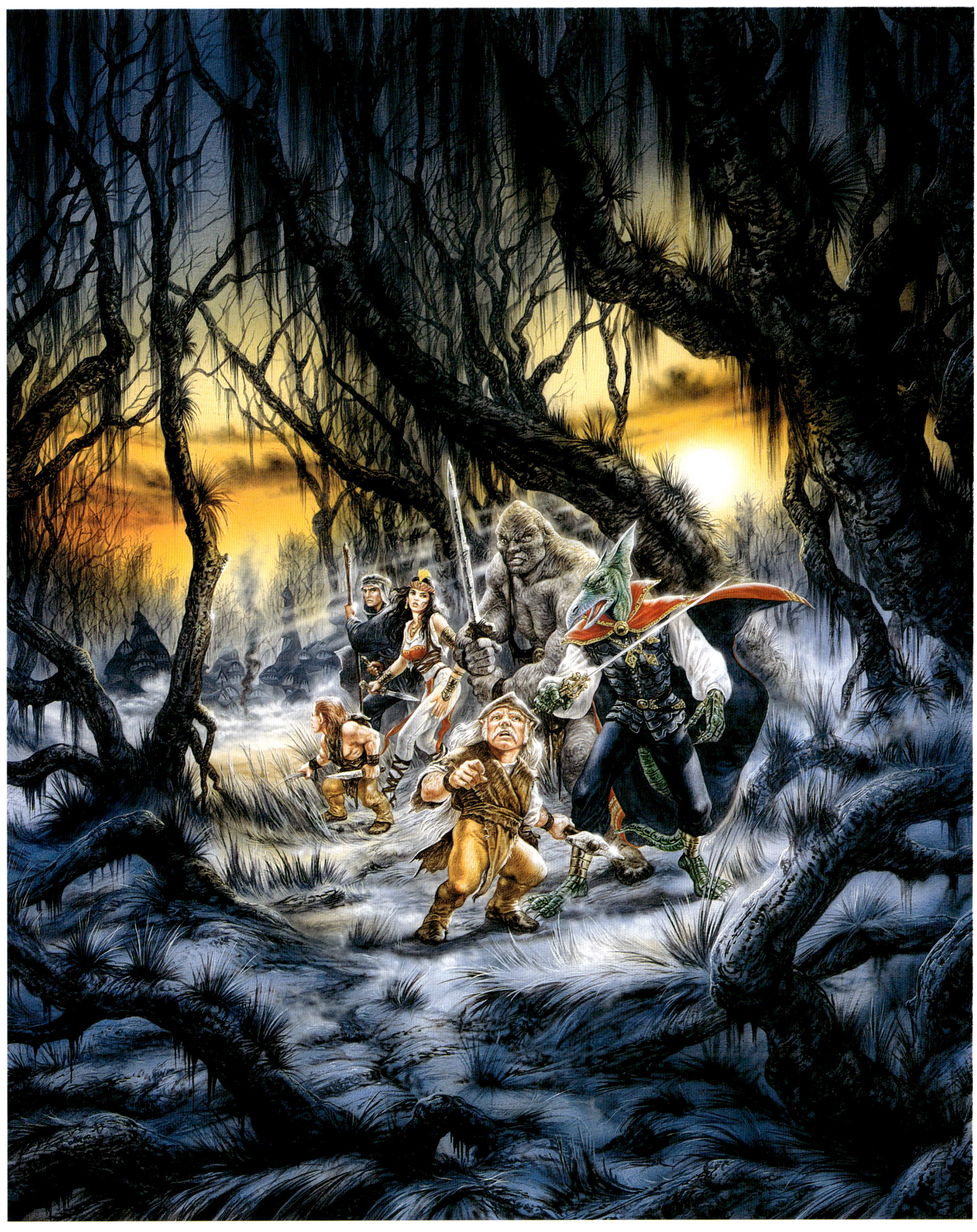

■ NINE TONGUES AND A TEAR

All the universe of illustration in one single point, a dominant color, a drop of blood that looks us right in the eye. Games of symmetry, symbols, whispers of breeze, and, in front of the background in motion, the quiet, challenging figure.

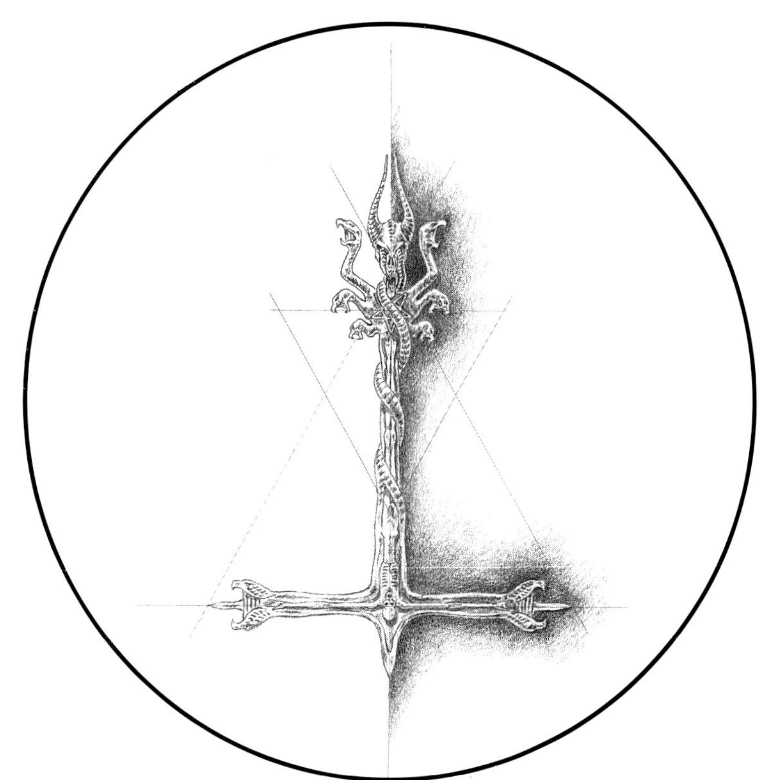

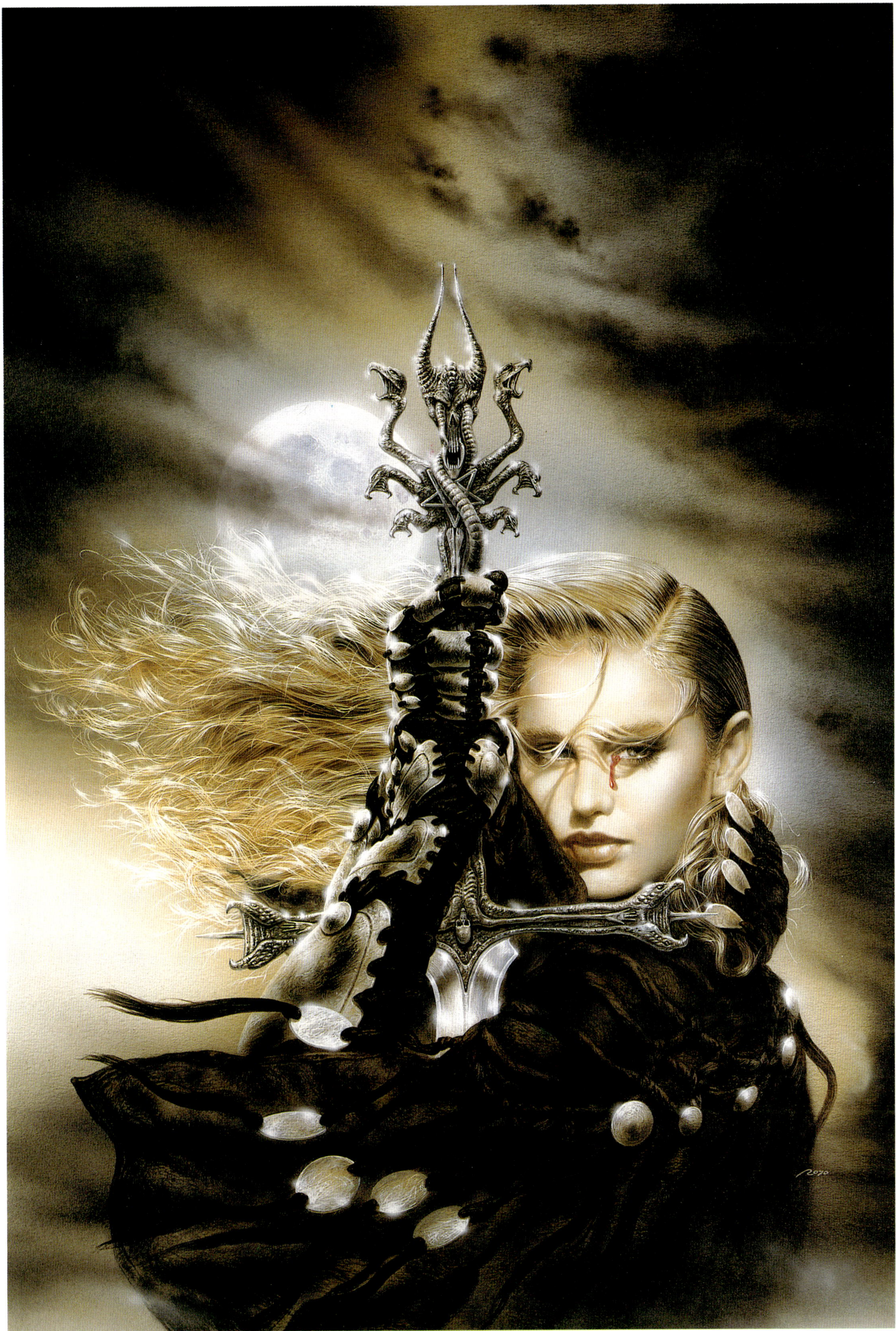

■ THE ROOFS OF FEAR

1993

Let the viewer feel exposed, out of place. Let him see himself as a menacing presence who upsets the balance of that paper architecture that can support huge rocks. An annoyance who, with his breath, can blow up a storm and pass sentence on the world of the unconscious.

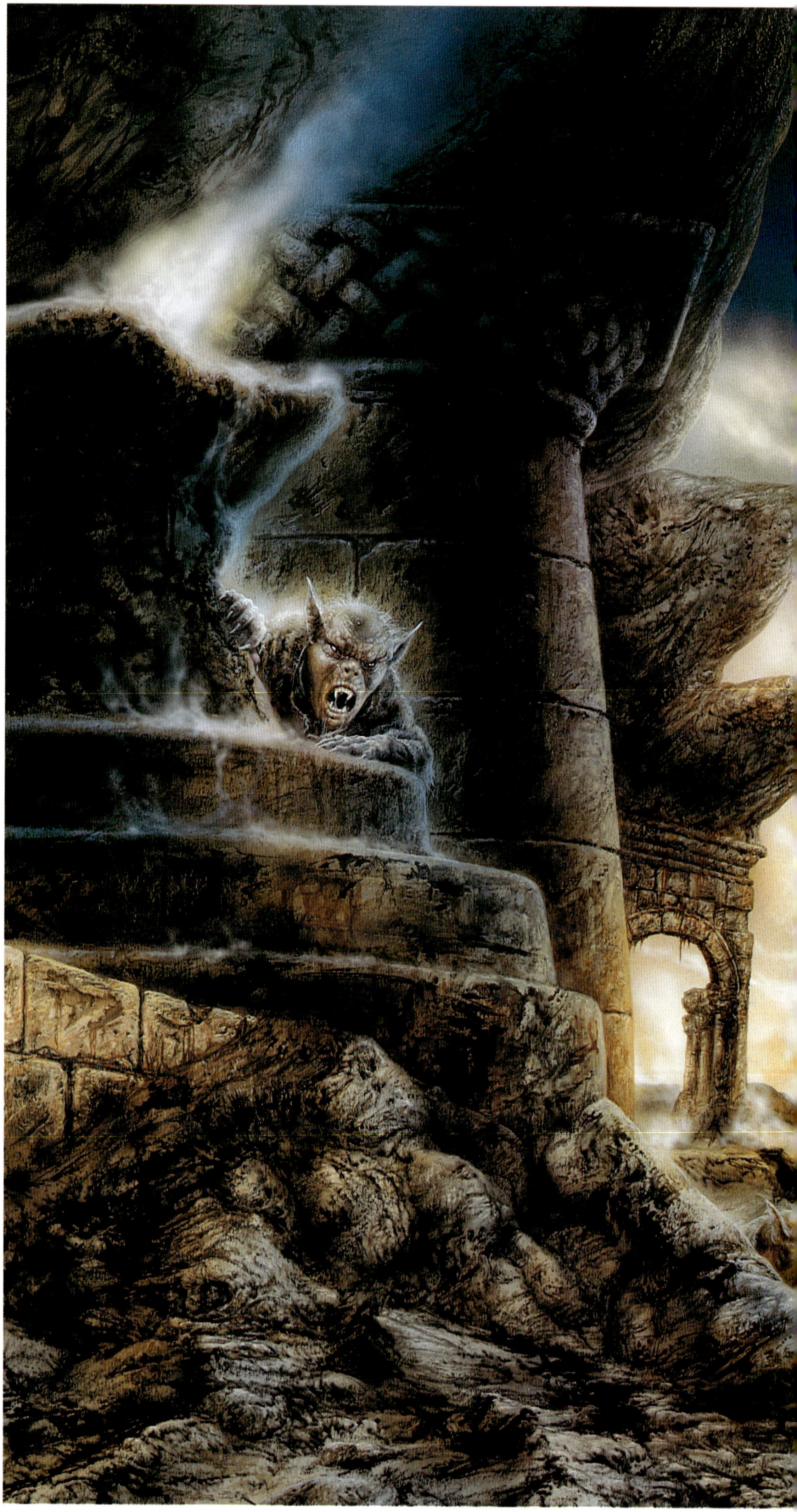

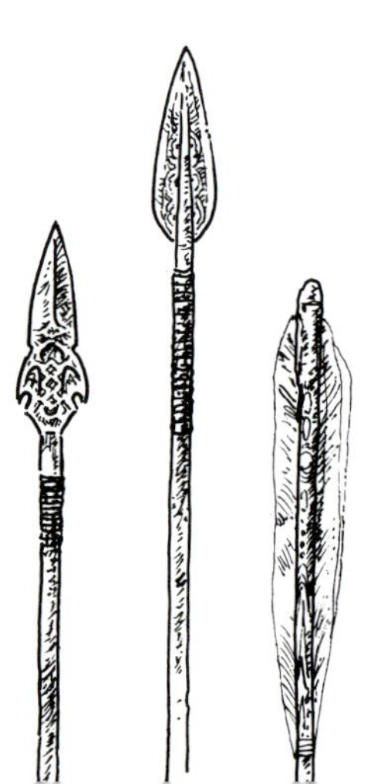

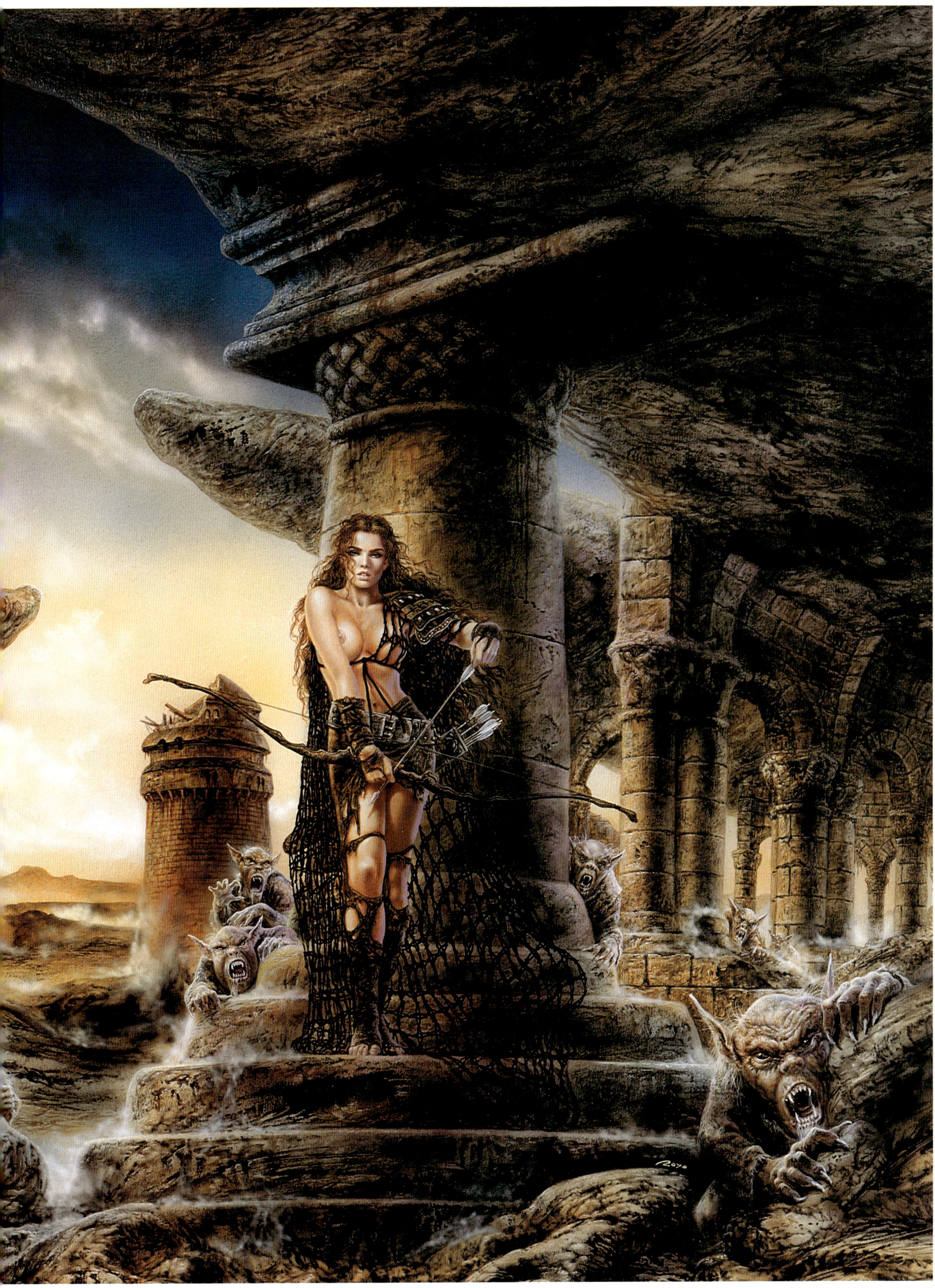
Royo

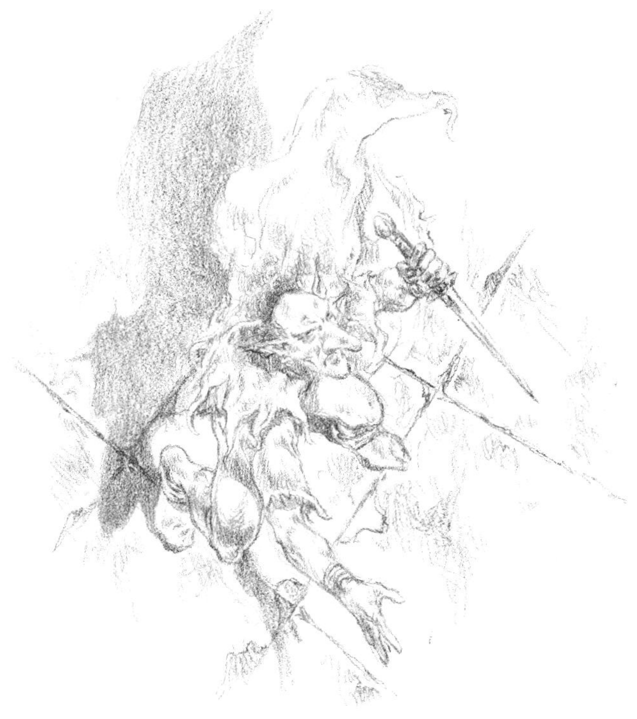

■ THE SUMMONING
1992
Point of view, vanishing point, shining point, magic point.
Playing games with circles as if they were drops of paint dripping from paintbrushes and creating forms on the bottom of a vase.

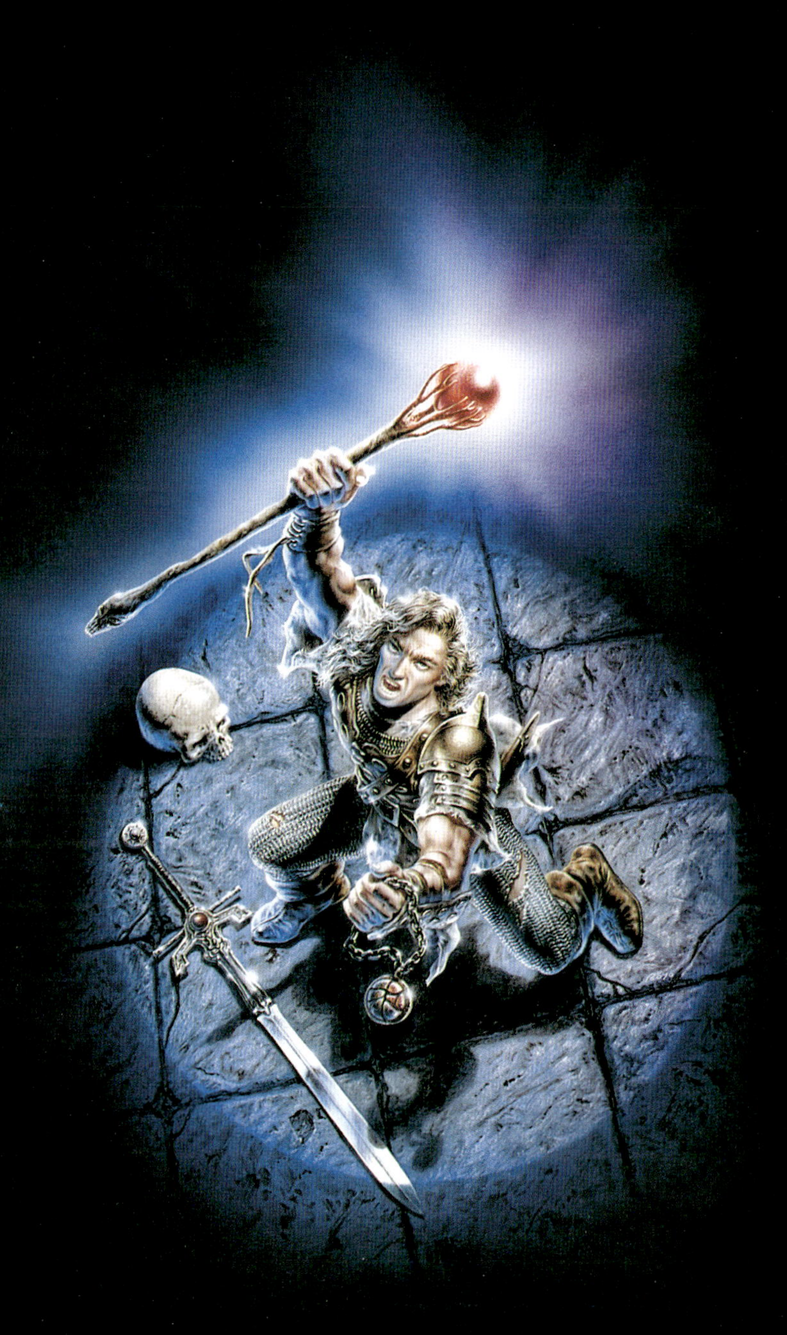

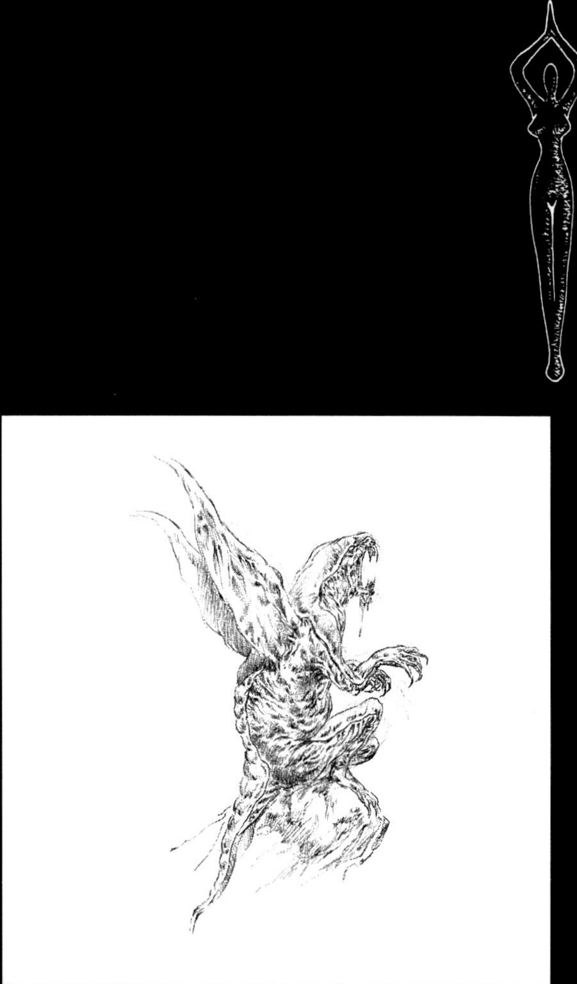

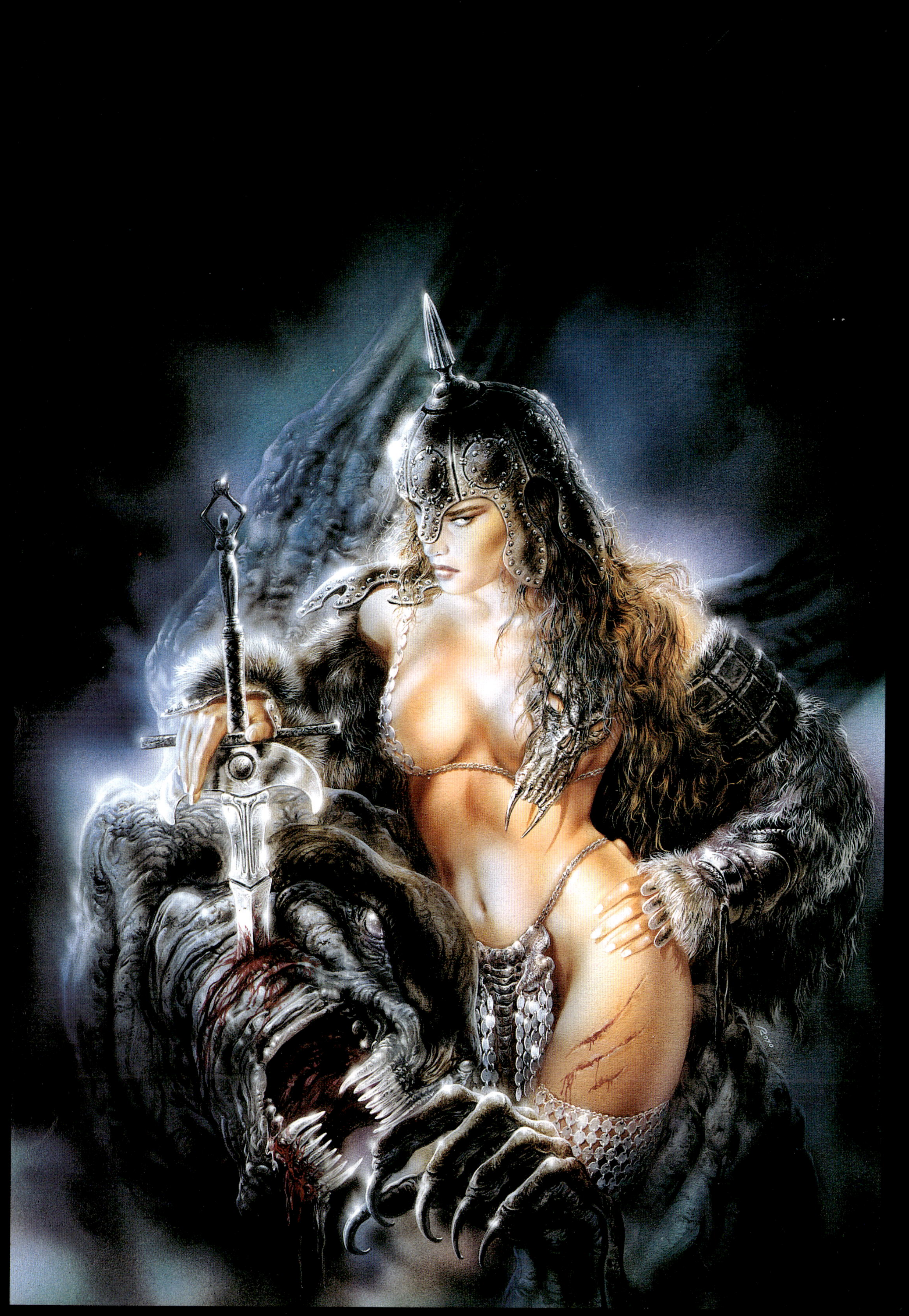

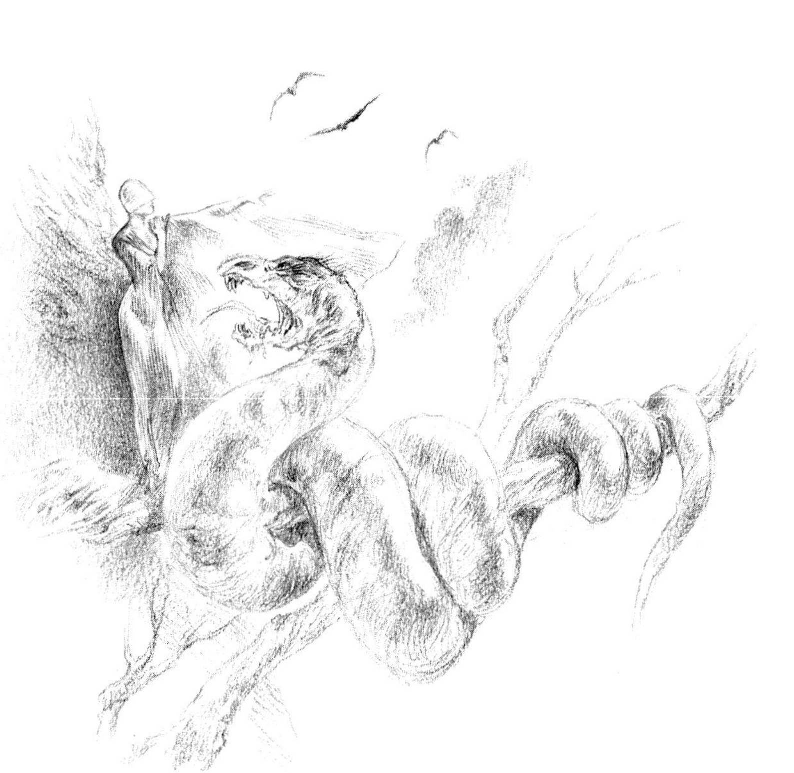

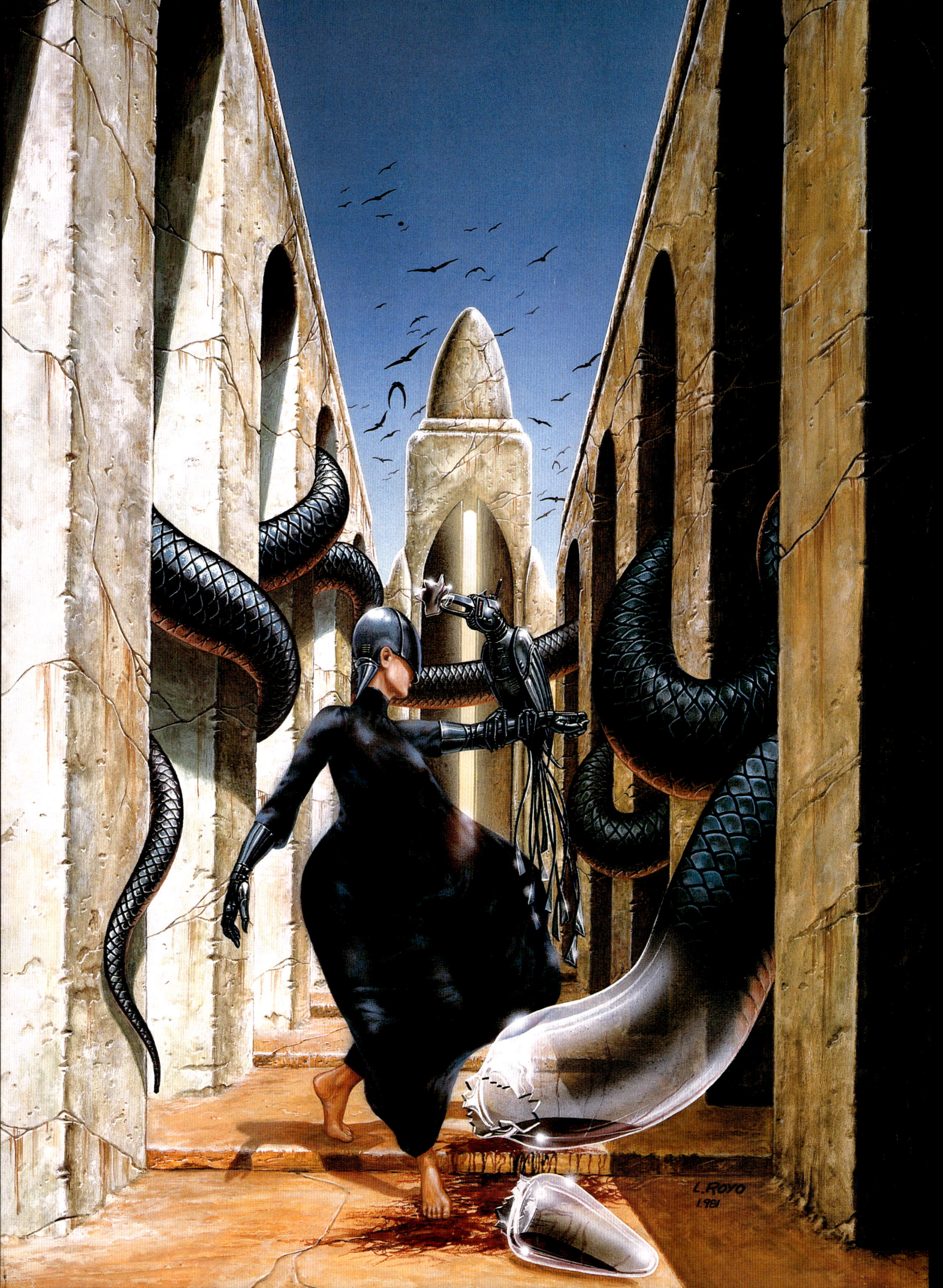
L.ROYO
1.981

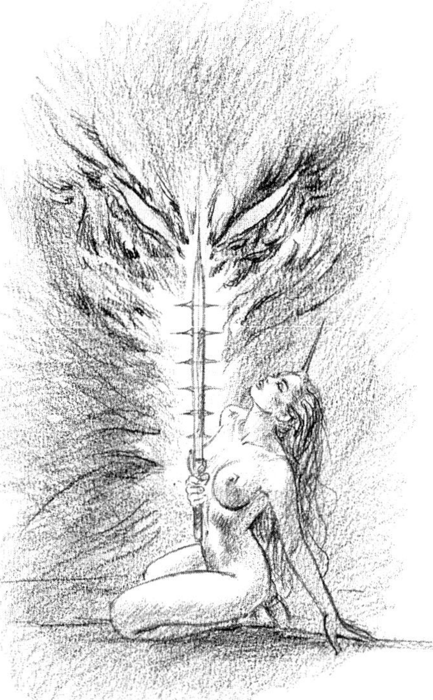

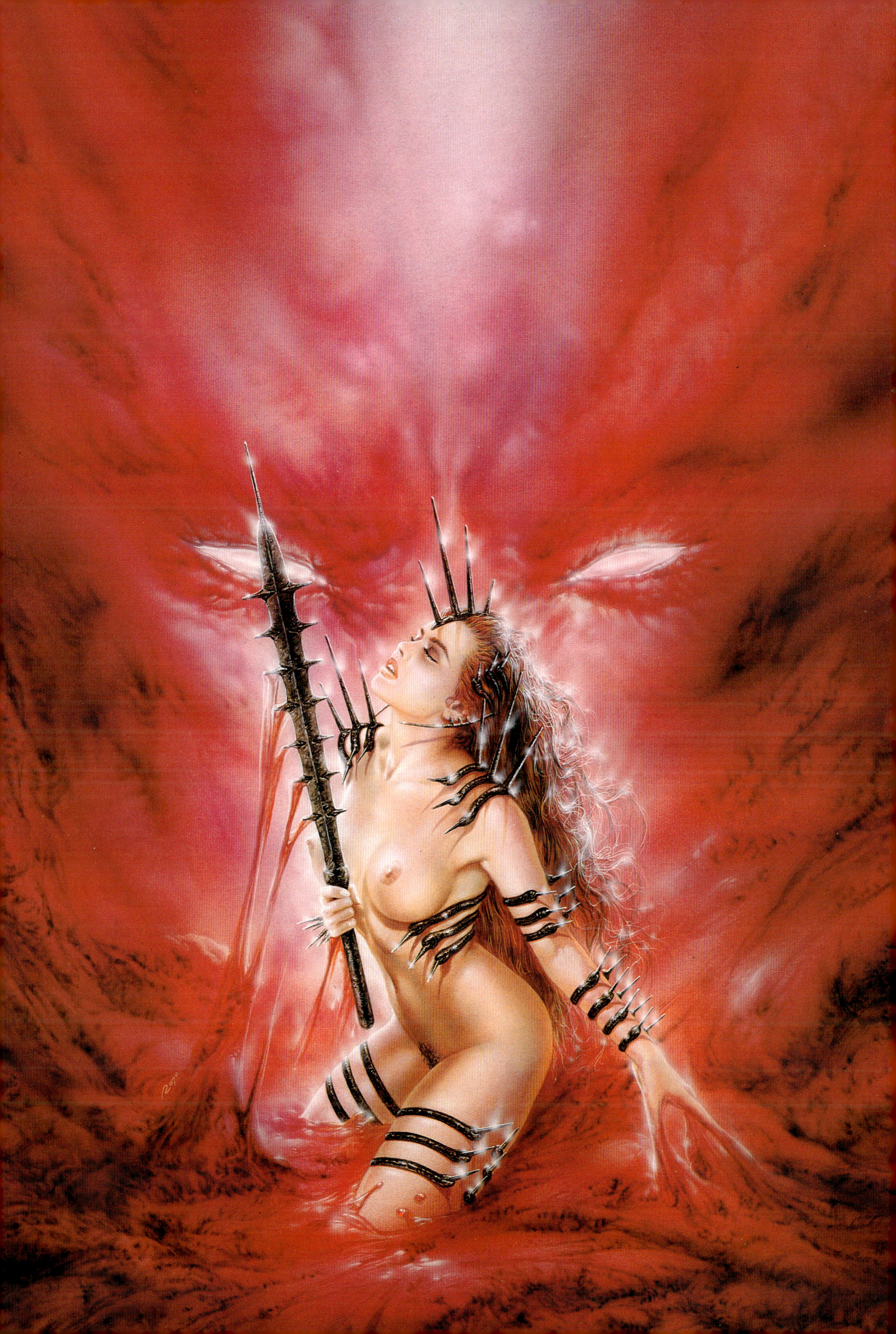

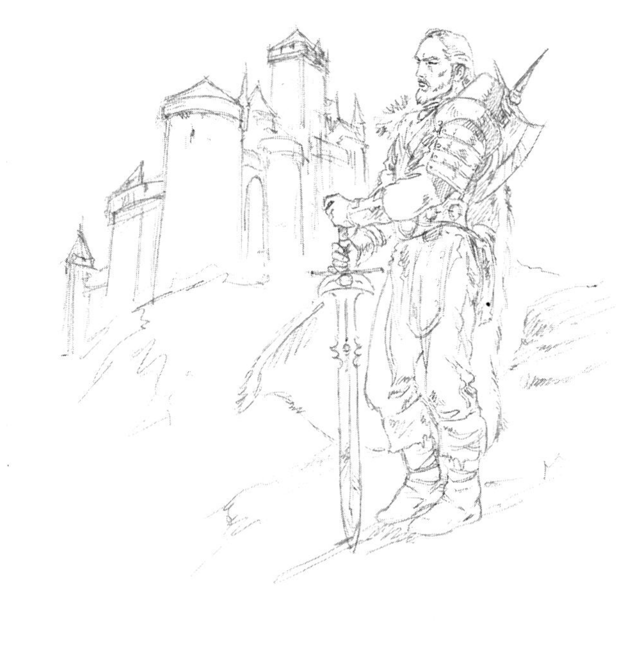

■ LEGEND
1994
Classic scene:
The powerful hero.
The enemies approaching.
The eternal castle.
The defiant sword.
From far off it becomes a cover that has what it takes to attract a reader.

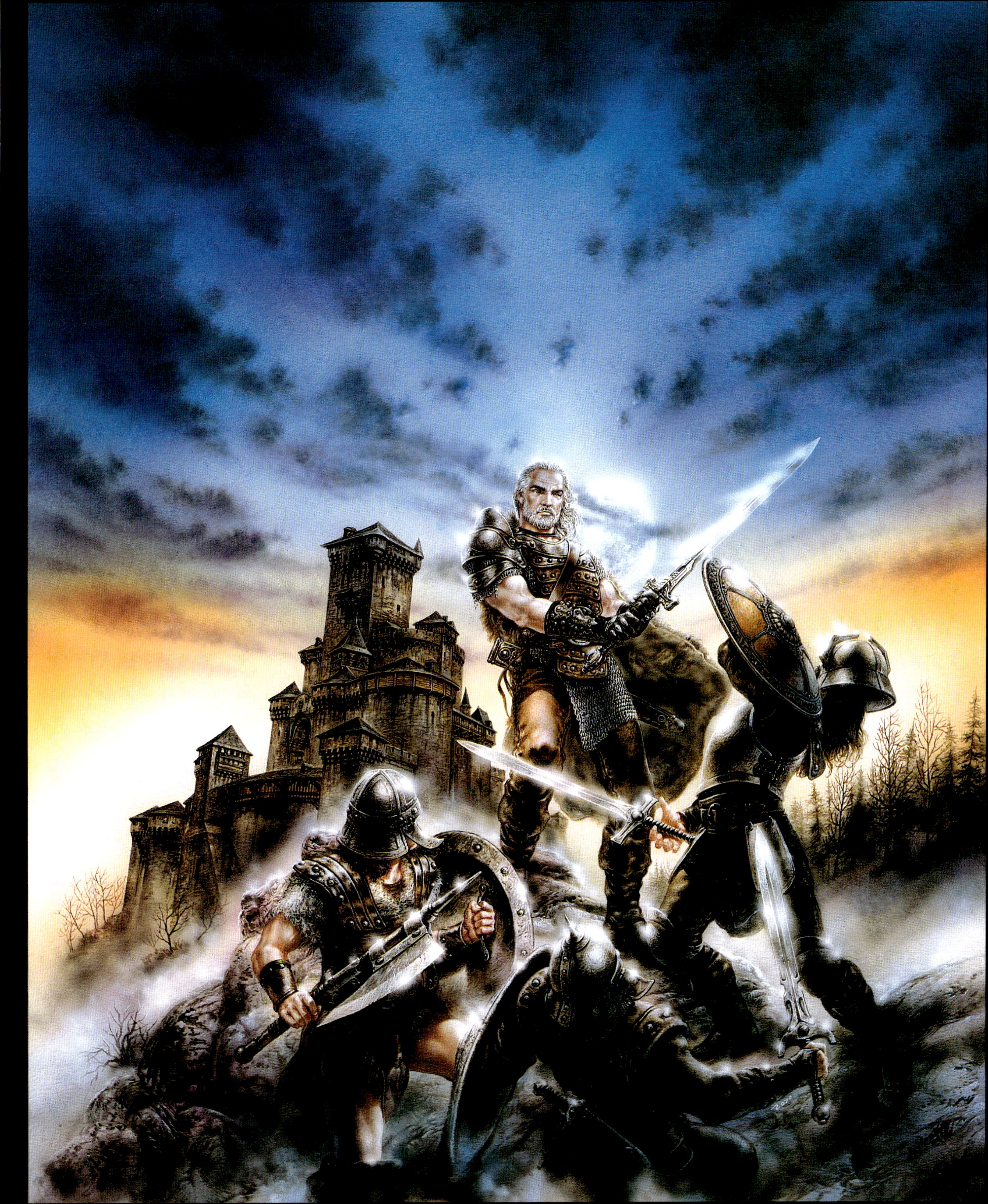

■ KISS OF THE FOG

1993

The art of evil. Not looking for perspective or contorsions. A simple, naked front view so as to feel the attraction of the perverse.

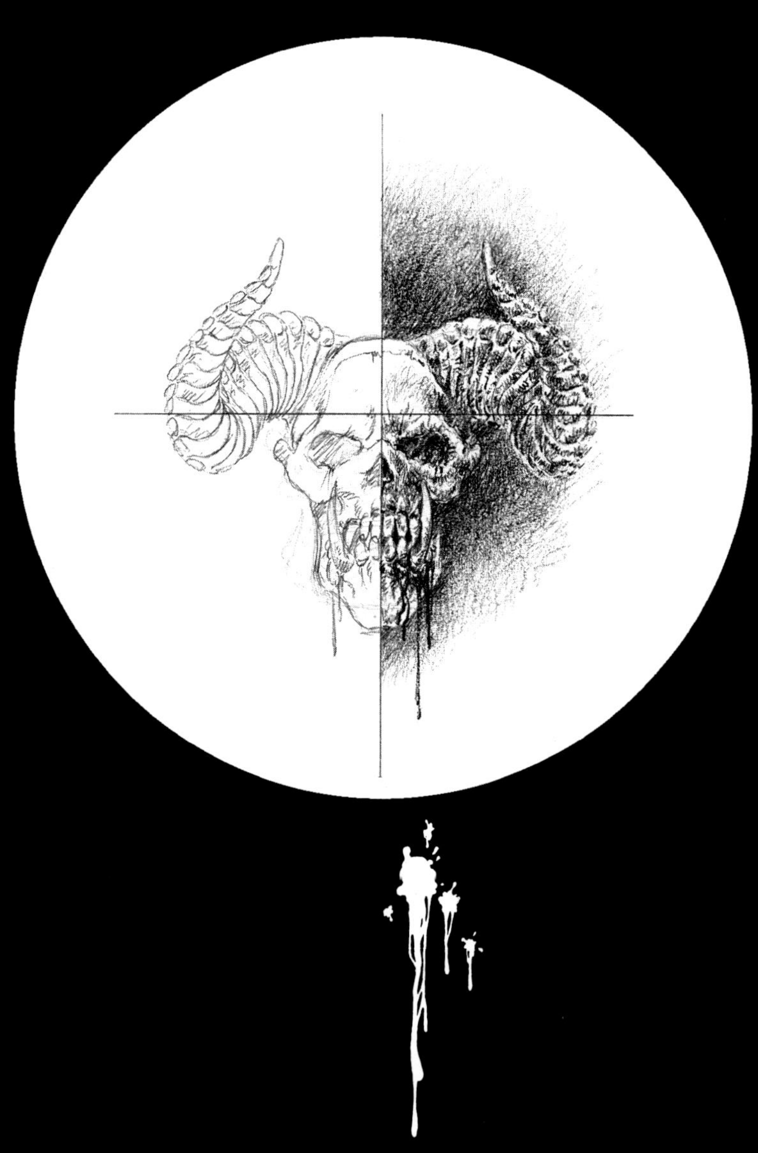

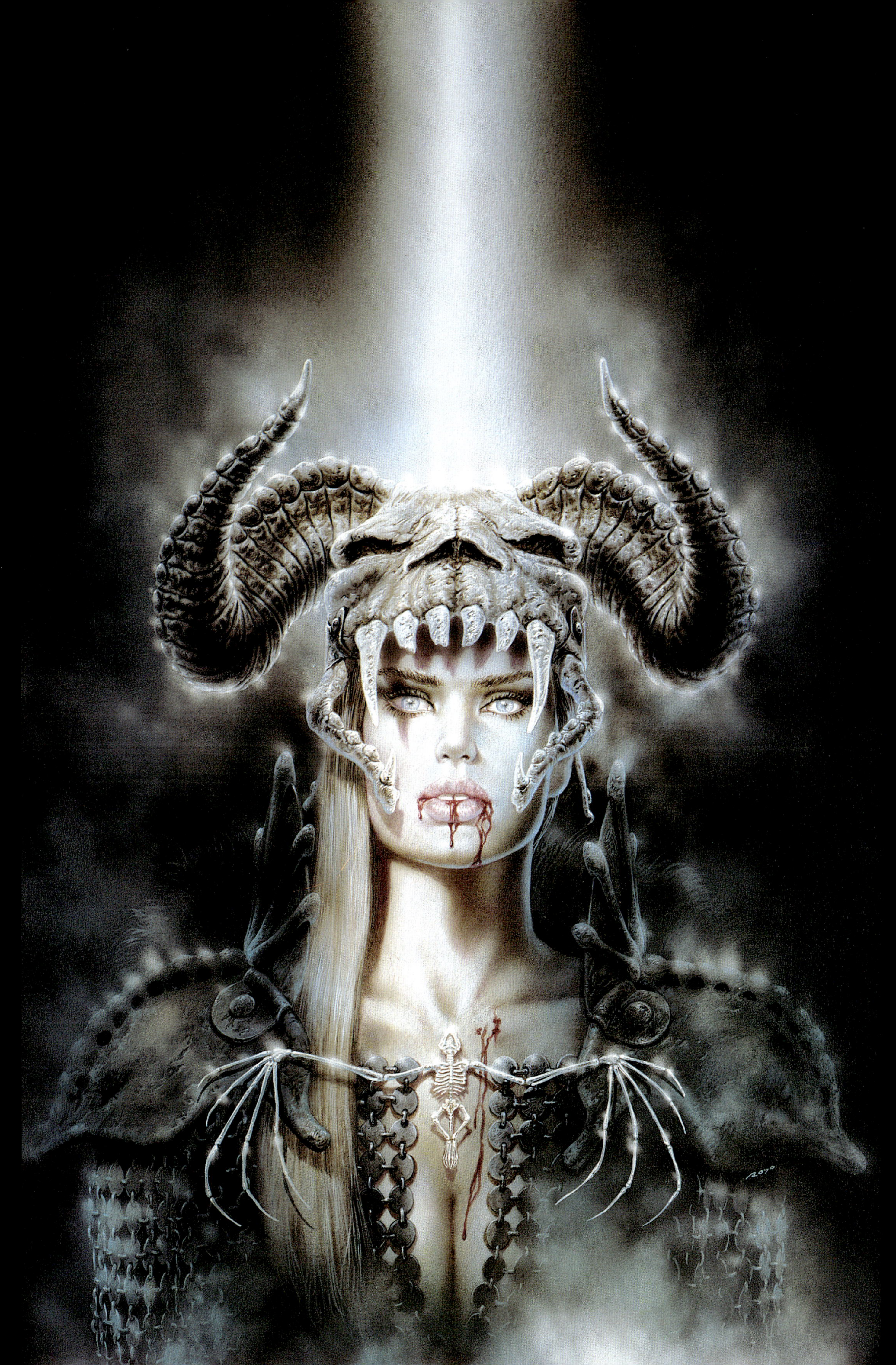

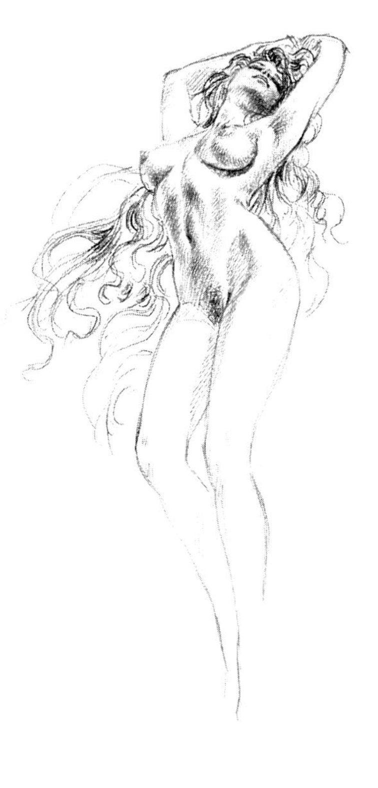

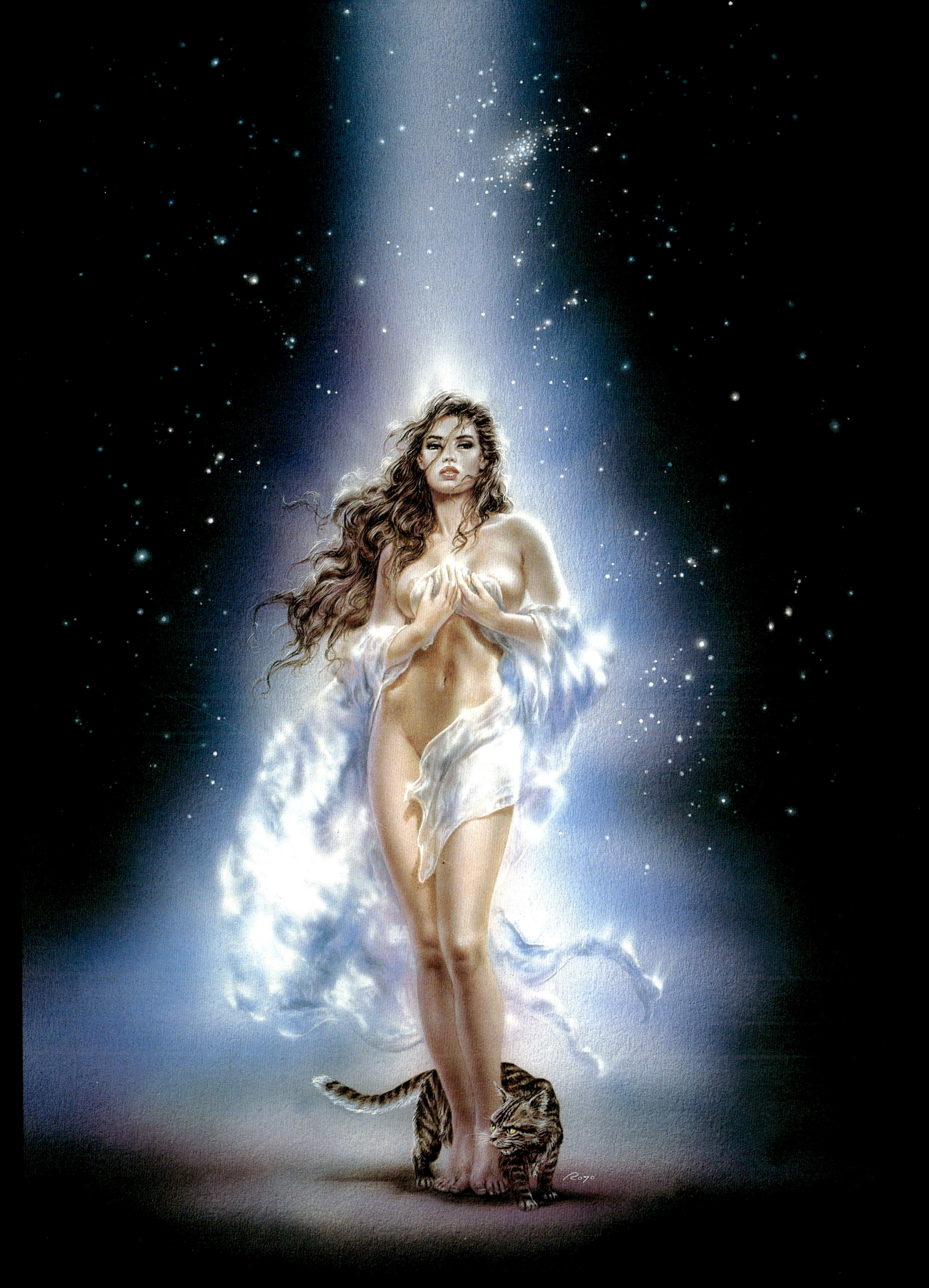
Royo

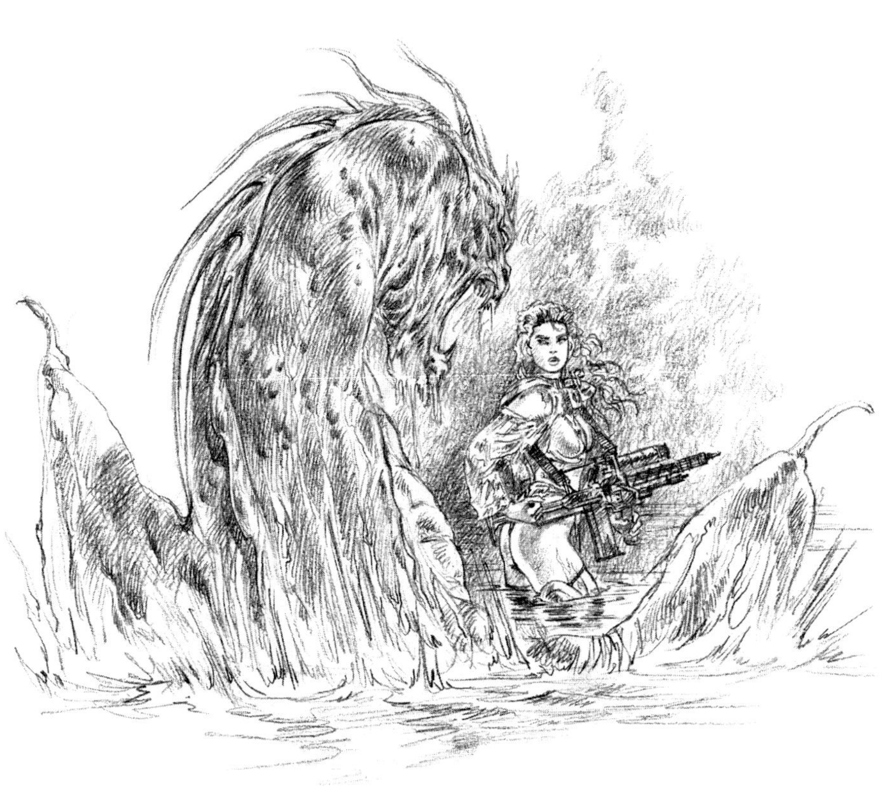

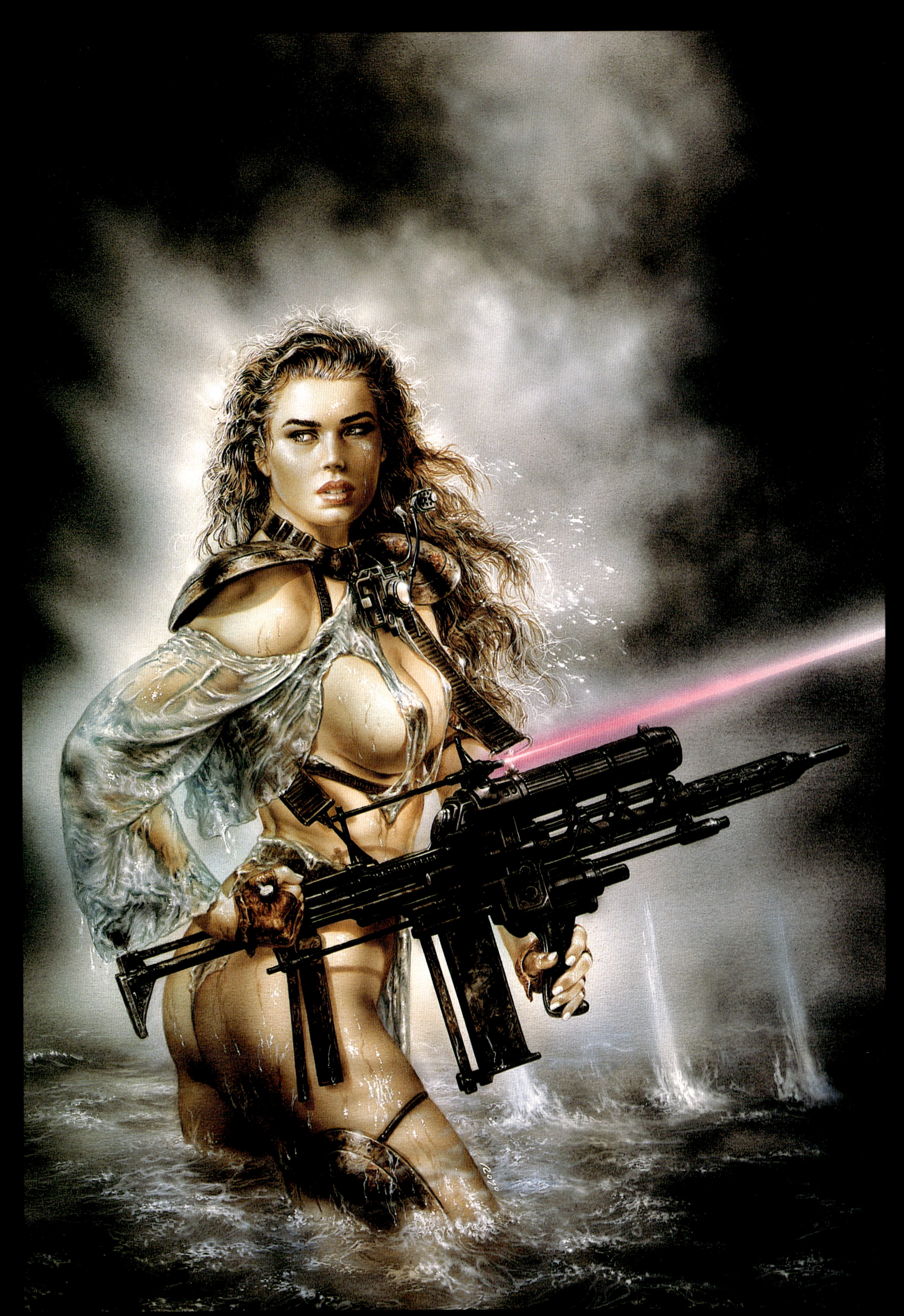

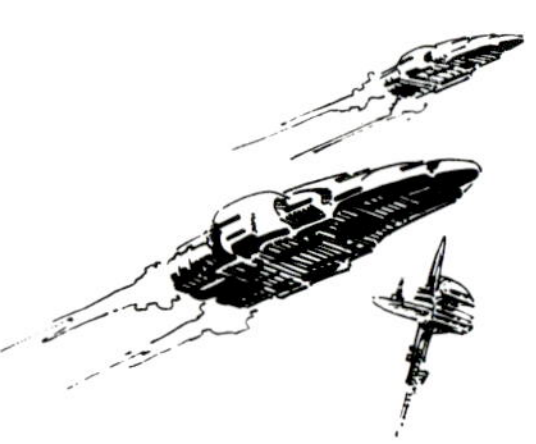

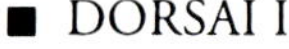

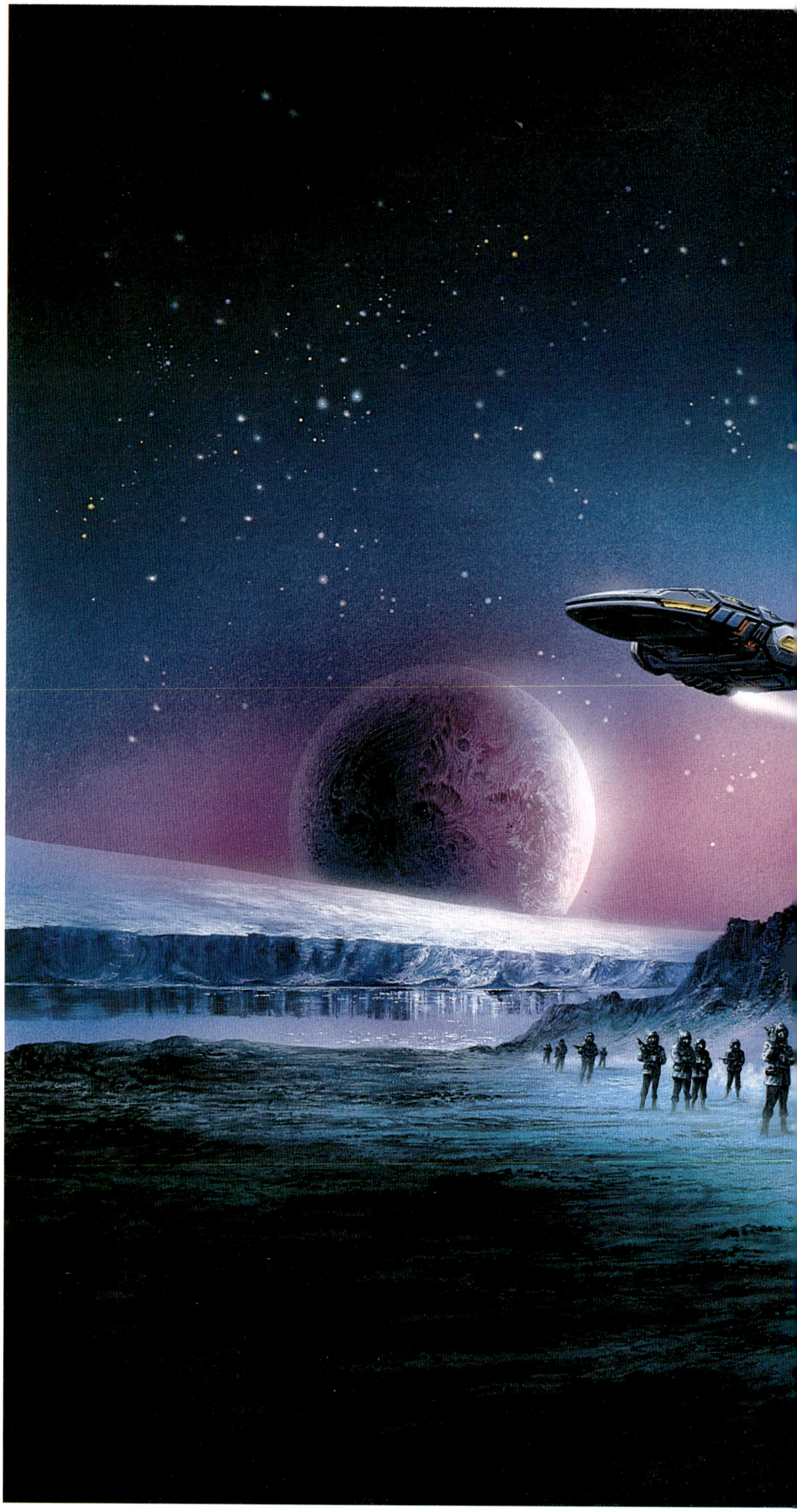

■ DORSAI I

1992

Today we can still take advantage of the knowledge of technique they had in the Renaissance. The classic triangle of composition with its symmetry and equilibrium, the arrangement of planes that gives characters their importance, and the architecture that frames it all and maintains balance.

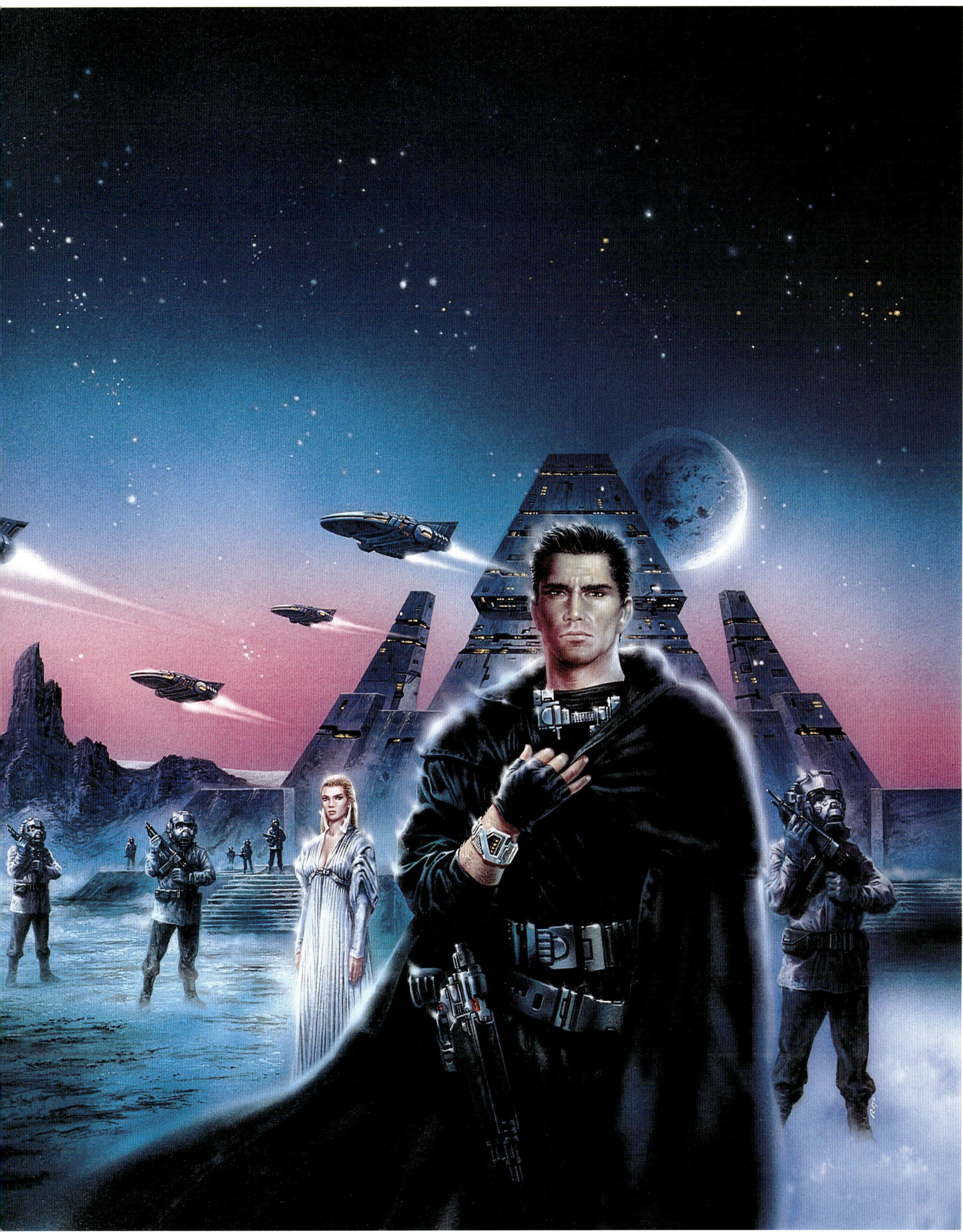

■ SPIRIT OF DORSAI

1992

An attempt to get the spirit down on paper. Characters from different periods of time shown in one image, but without the heroine losing her importance or her central position in the scene.

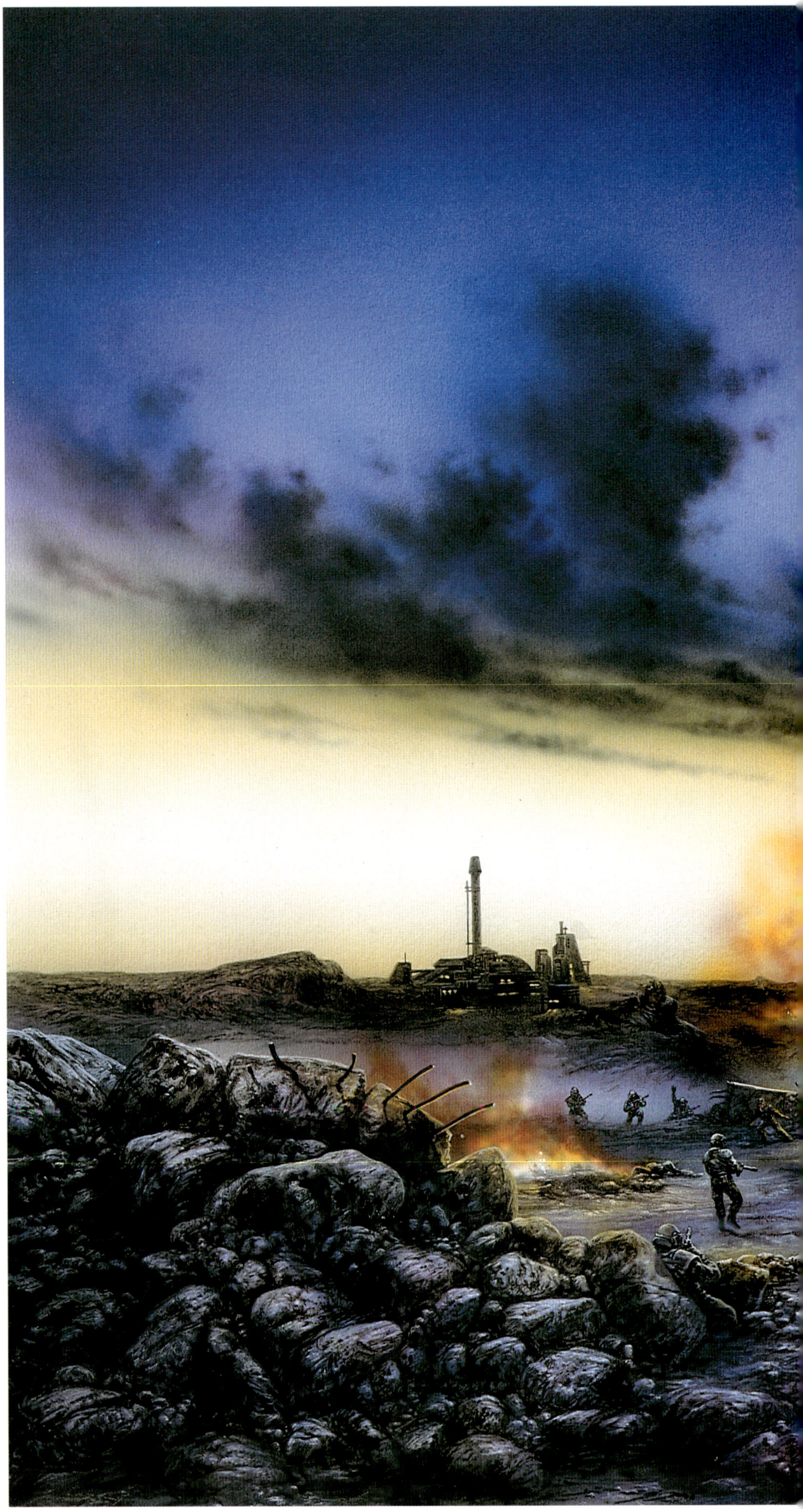

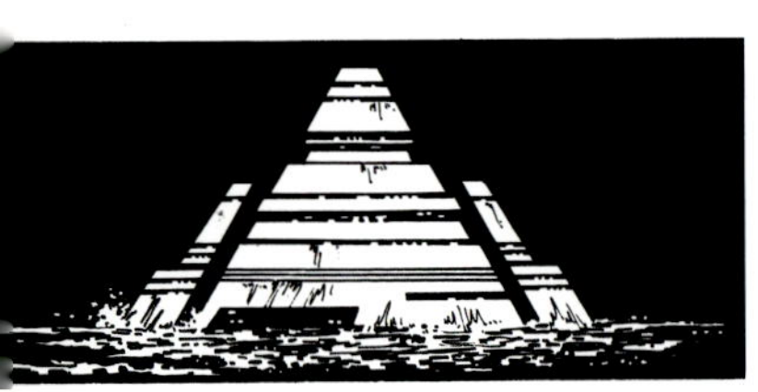

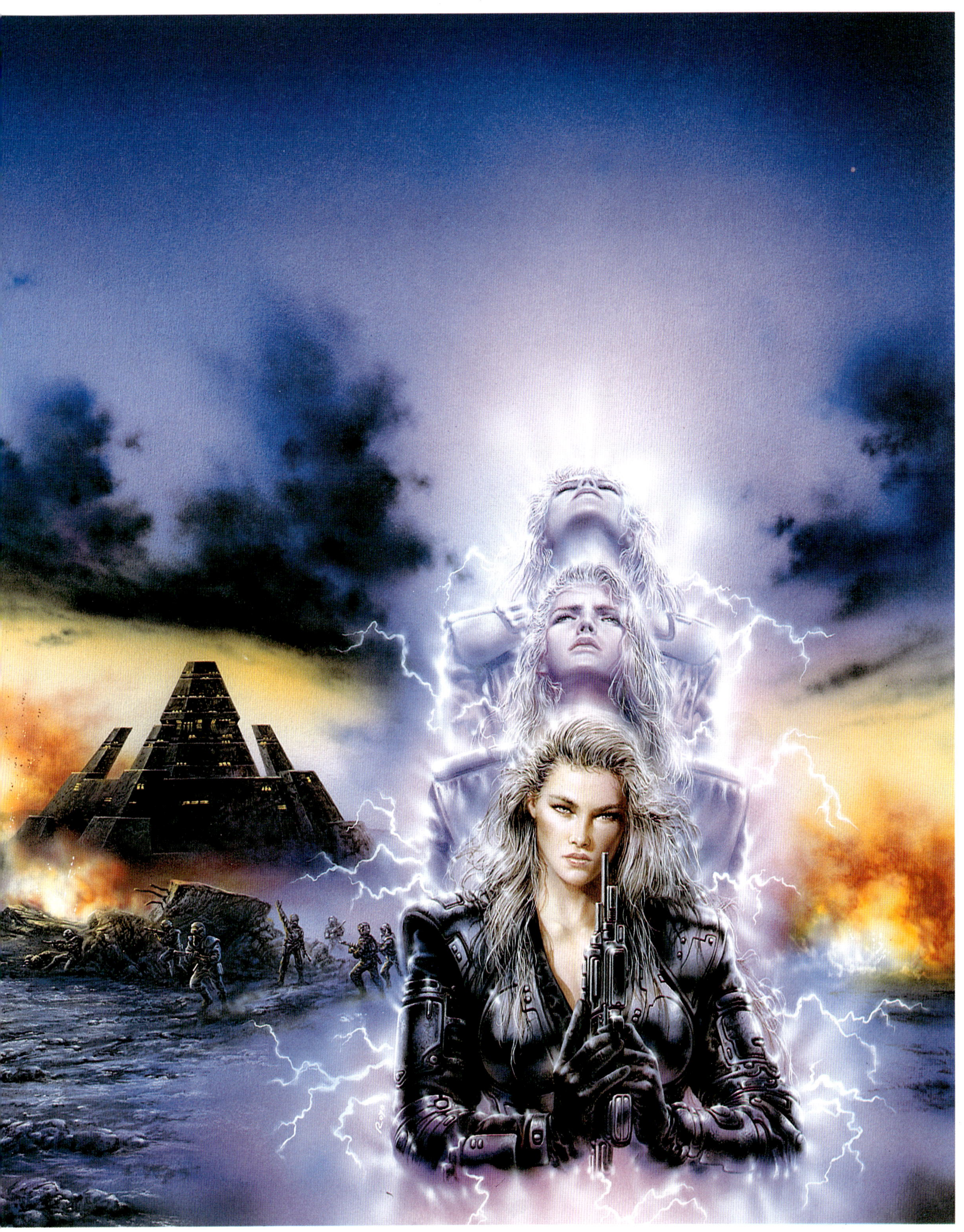

■ THE NEVER-ENDING SPARKLE

1993

Innocence--wickedness. On her knees--victorious. Relaxed--threatening. The face of a little girl--the look of a serpent. The breasts of a damsel--the sword of a fierce warrior. The end of one battle--the beginning of another. The vertical light of a cathedral--the dark circle of a sewer.

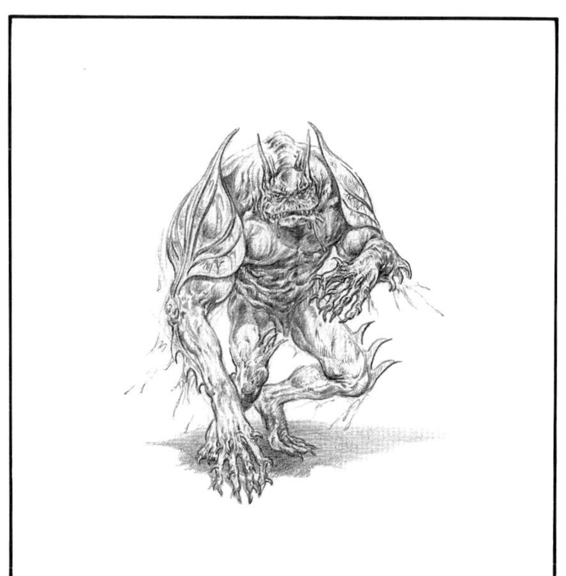

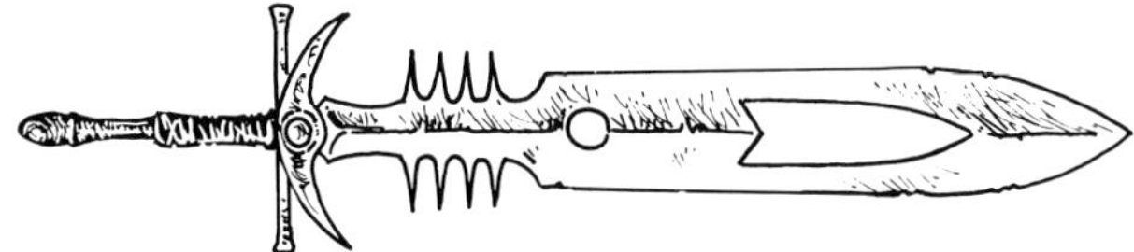

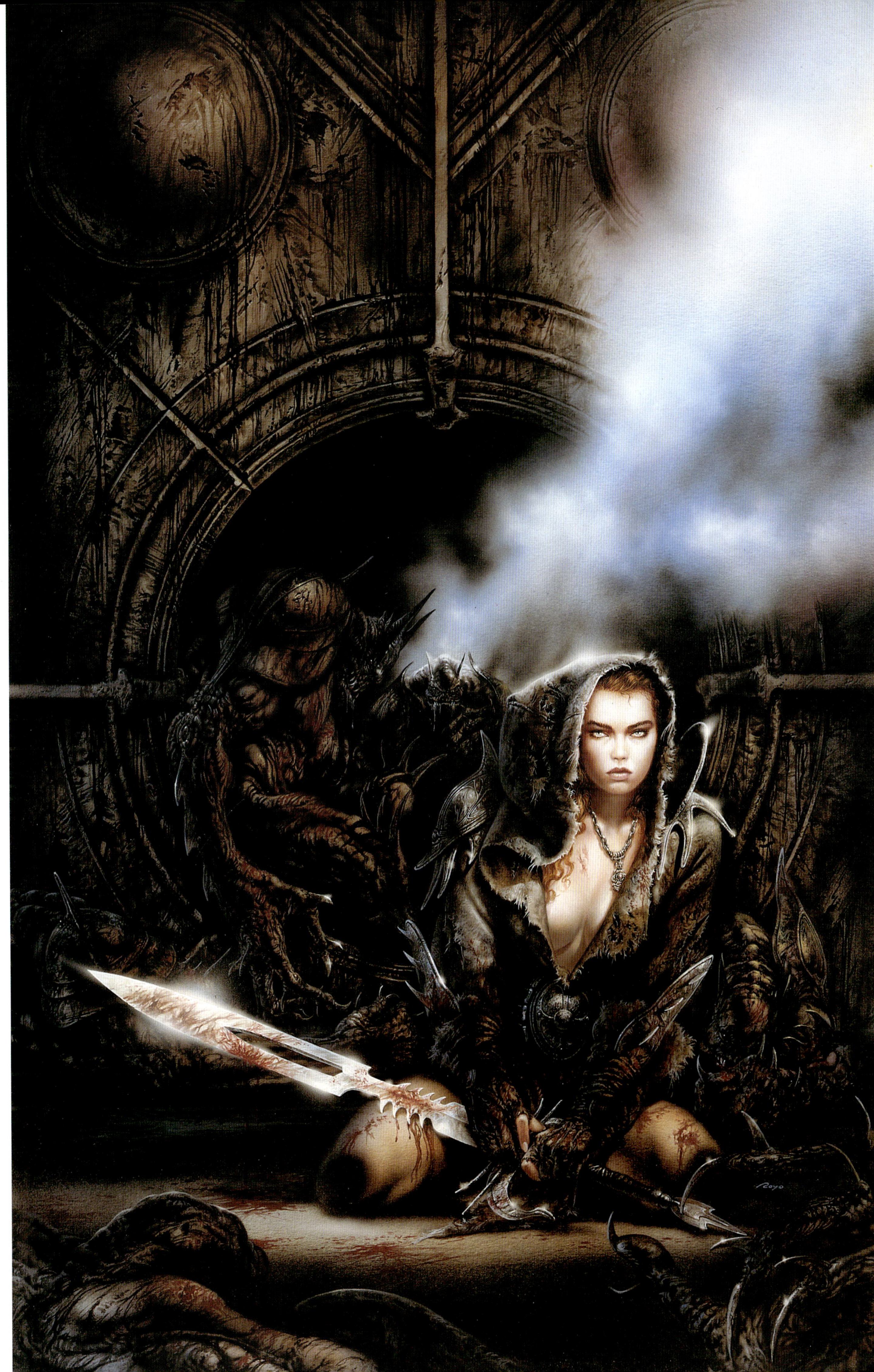

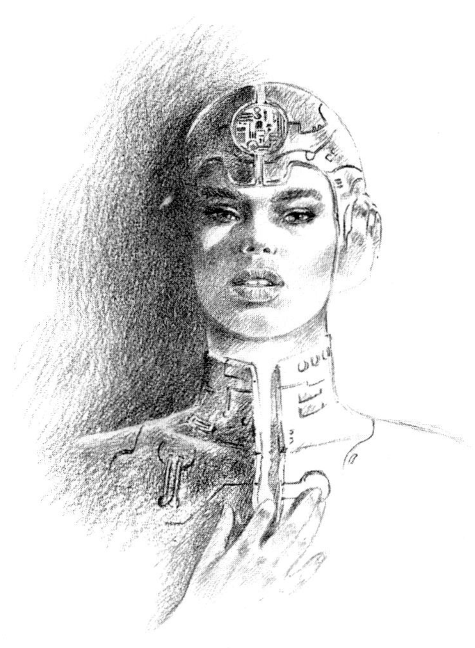

■ NEW SKIN

1992

A shriek of colors.

A nearness that invites you to scrape it with your teeth. A silhouette lost in sparkles. And the feeling that your eyes can't see it all, that outside the image there's a more passionate scene that we're forbidden to see.

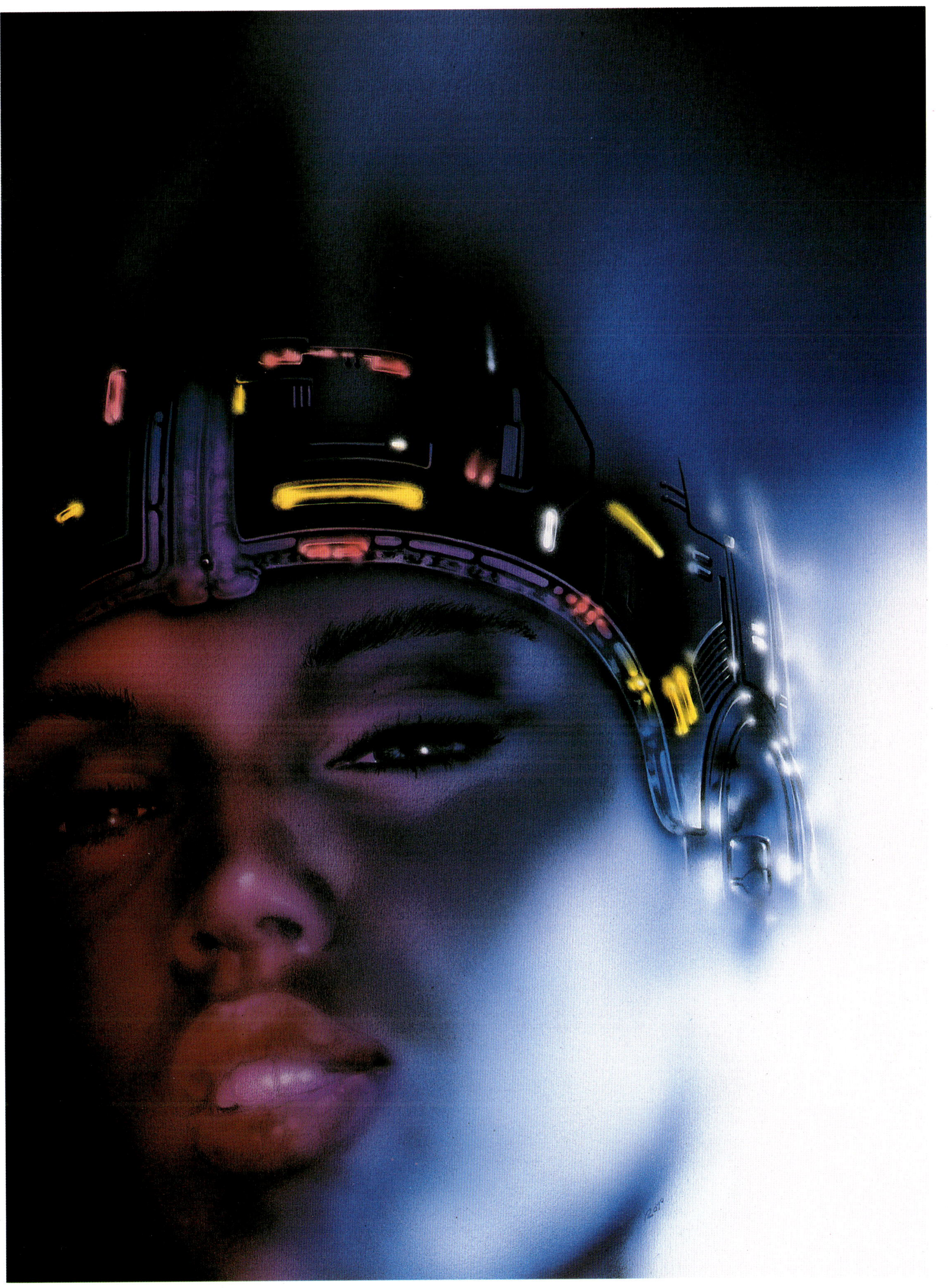

■ DEATH DREAM
1987
An equator that divides North and South, the past and the future, flesh and metal, order and chaos, oneness and multiplicity.
Syrup for the eyes, served ice cold.

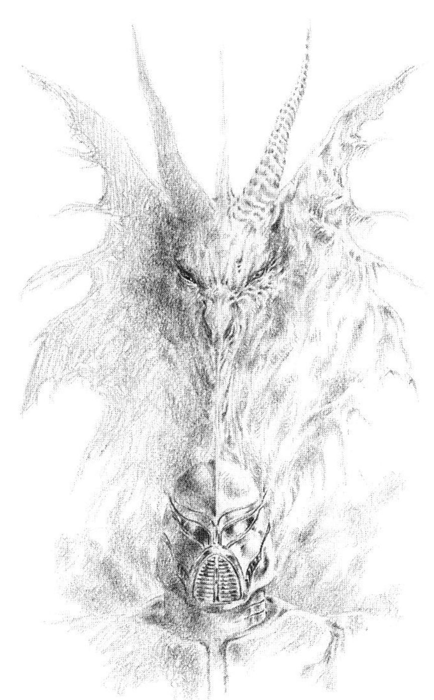

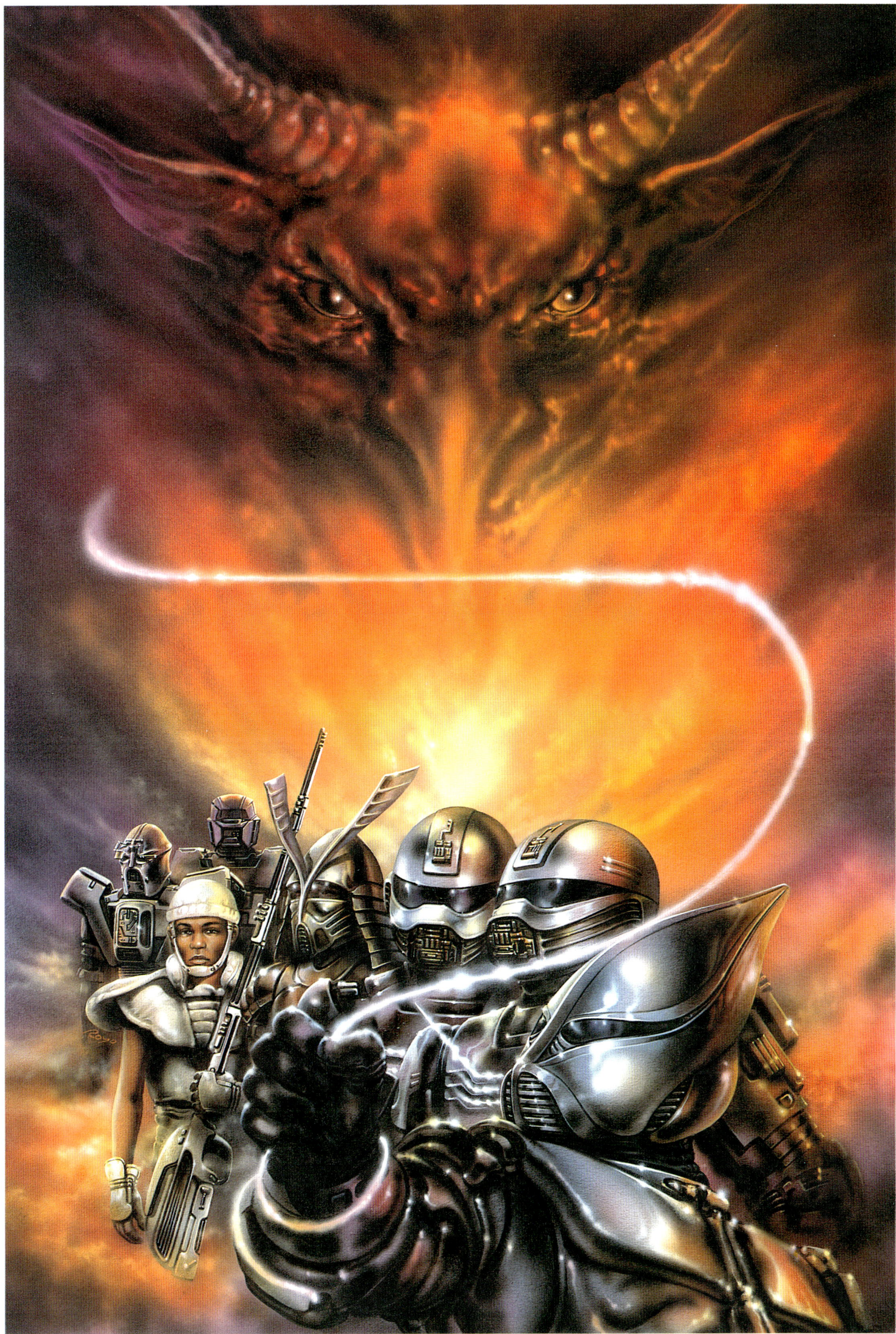

■ STEEL FOR LEONARDO'S DREAM

1992

If metal is sharp, let it cut the air.
If wings let you fly, fly with the signs of the zodiac.
If feathers caress, let them produce wounds.
If fire makes images lose their outline, let it delineate the horizon.
If the eye captures the light, let it throw it back out...

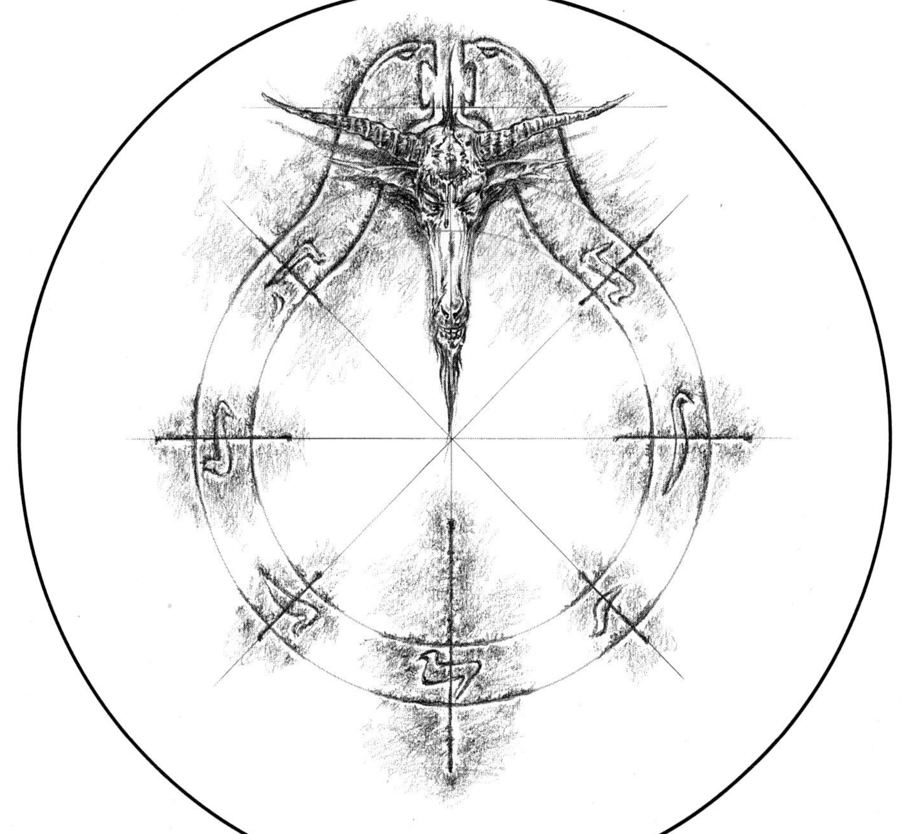

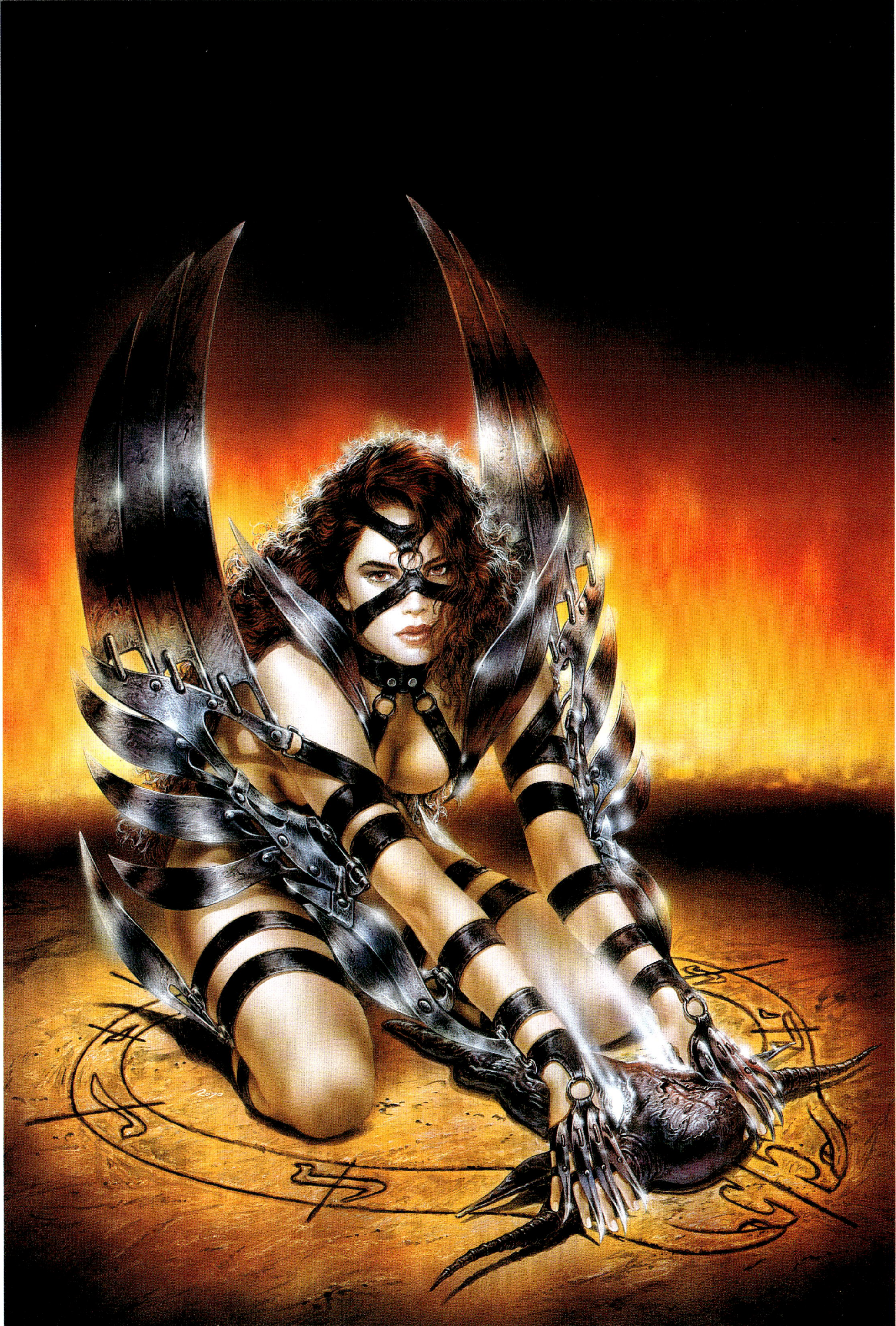

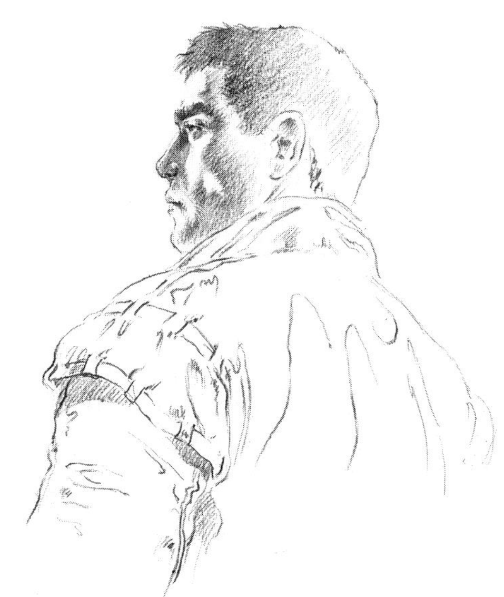

■ THE FIRST DUELIST

1993

Vertical steel to divide up space, to separate the world you live in from his, to put distance between his arrogance and you, to challenge you to see the world through his eyes, to separate your view of the present the way he separates his right hemisphere from his left.

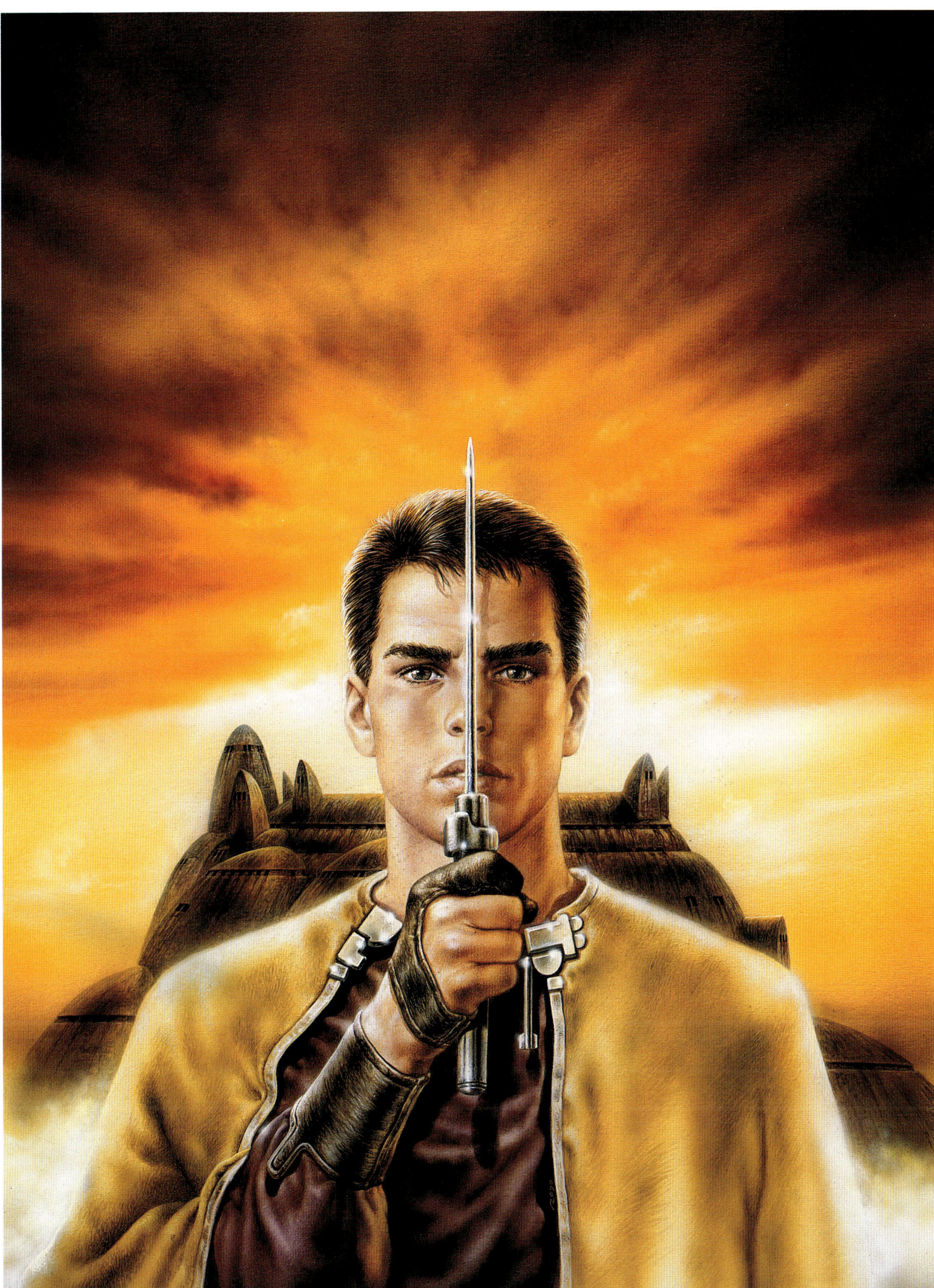

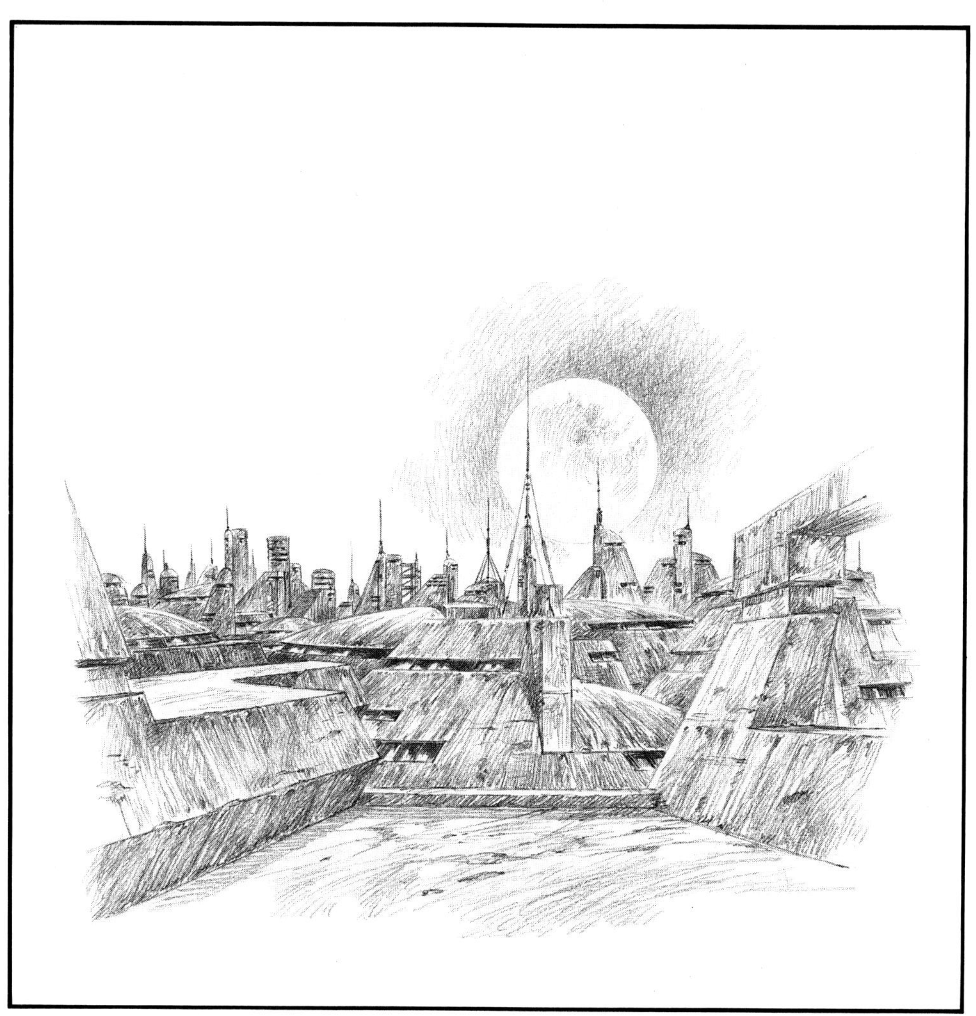

■ 2041

1993

Blue-green, mixed together and melted into one false color; the dwellers in the future have their windows filled with a yellow so furious it hurts to look at it.

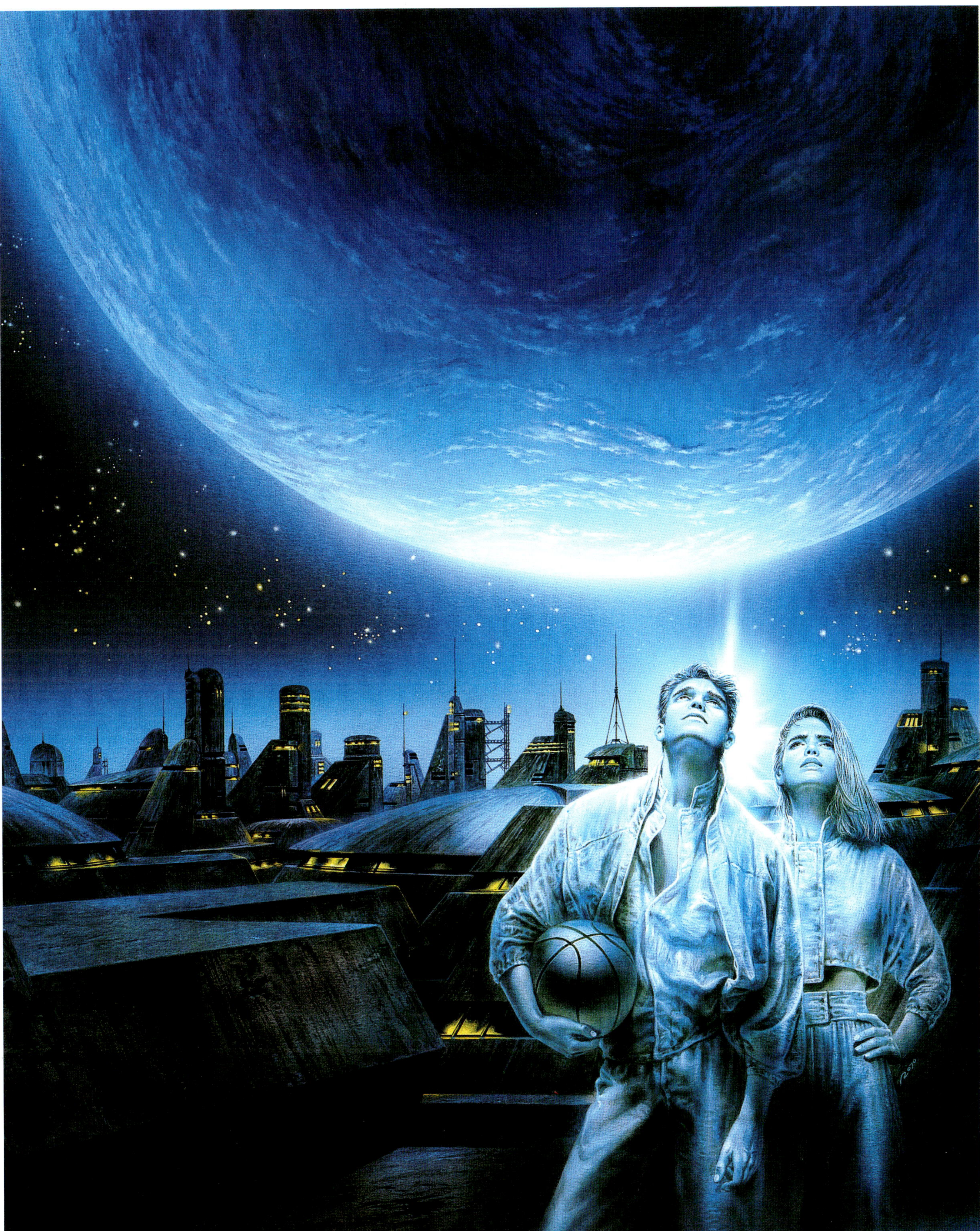

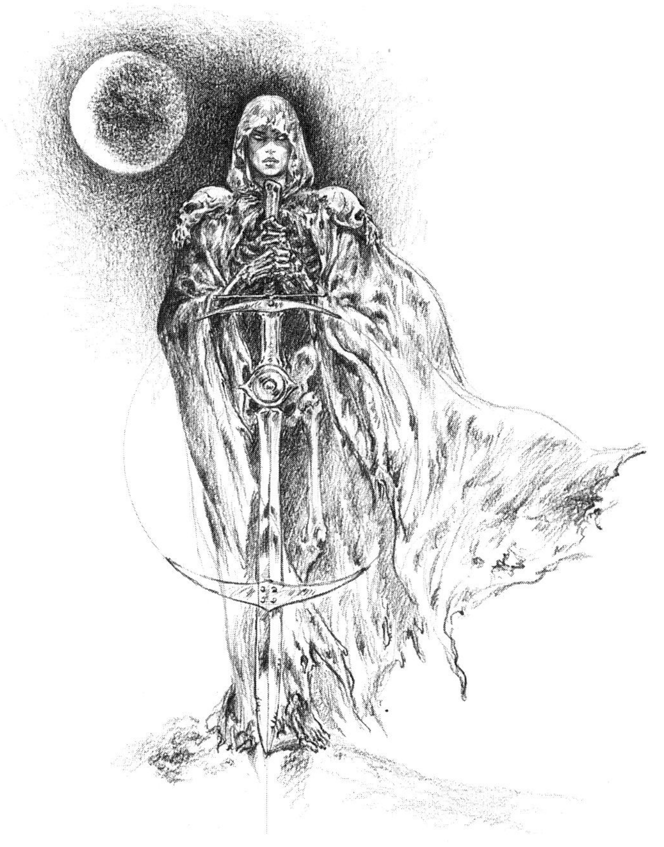

■ PAST-FUTURE FOG
1992
We dispense with the usual palette of colors and fill our fingertips instead with fog and let it flutter across the paper.
Point of departure: DEATH-SEX.
We give free rein to our subconscious fantasies: we paint the scythe as a sword, Death as the supreme female, and the skulls are the same as the brand-new machines. This can only be illustrated in gray.

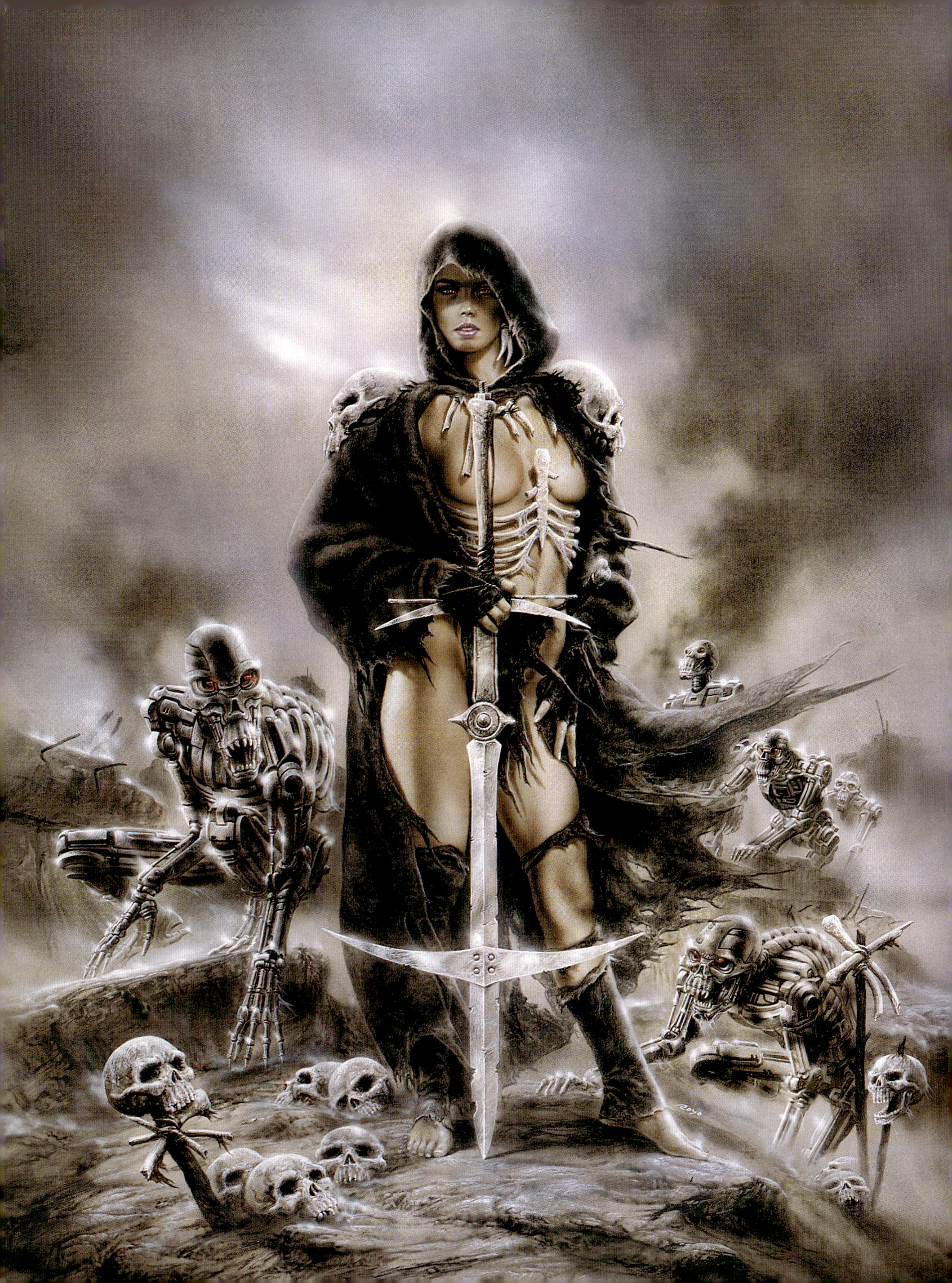

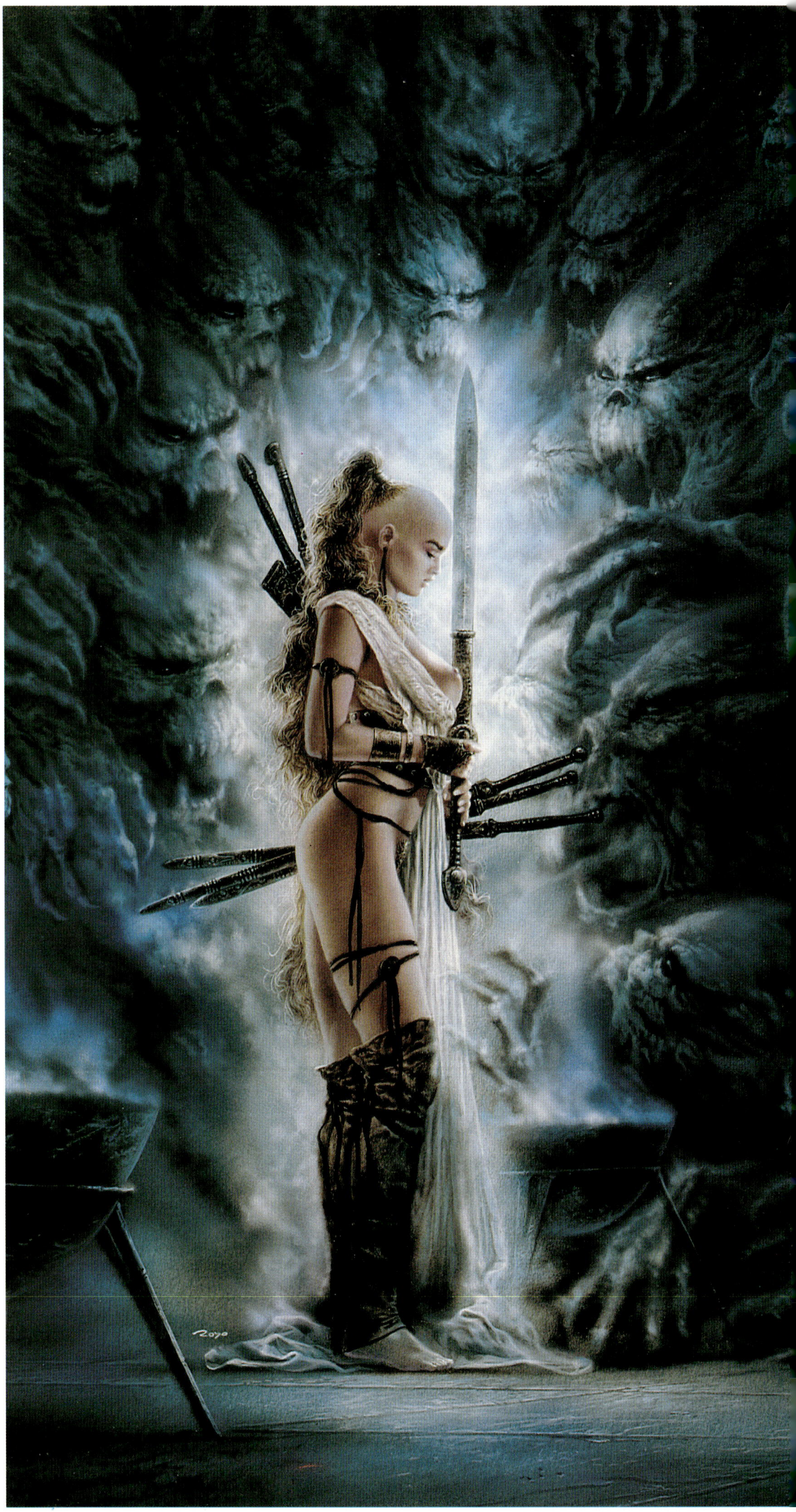

■ HOWLS OF SILENCE

1994

Cramming a lot of gestures and movements into a space so as to arrive at the borders of the baroque. Meanwhile, in the solitude of meditation, the tension of an indefinable color. To confront the void with an excess, and movement with equilibrium.

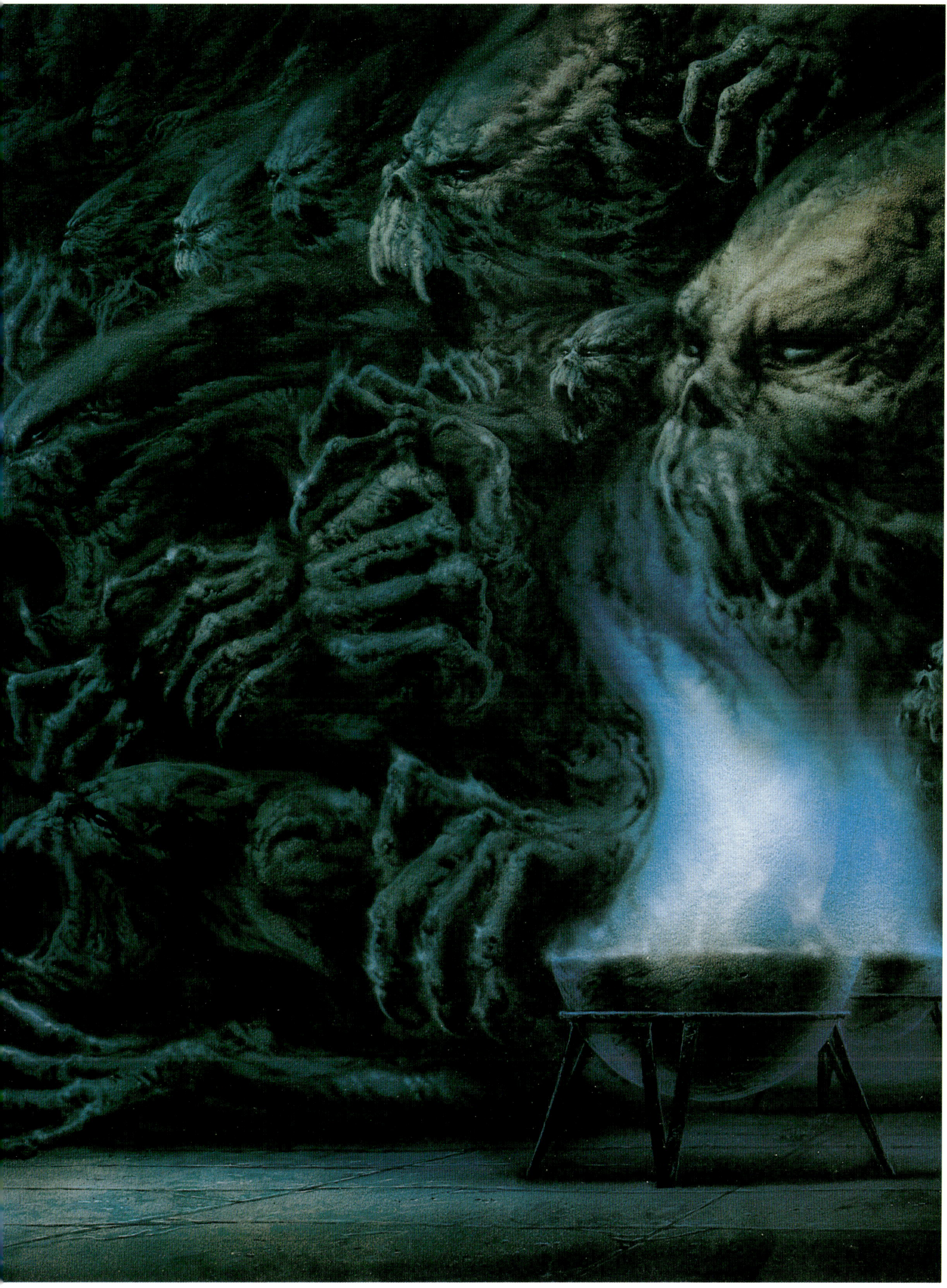

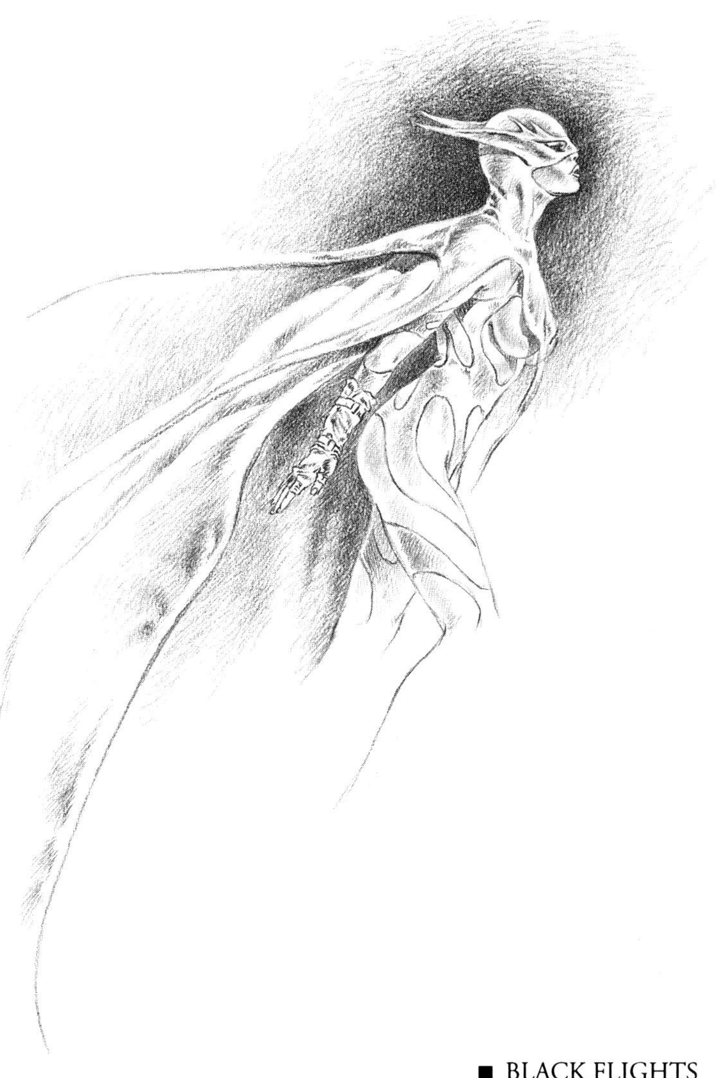

■ BLACK FLIGHTS

1992

Man repeated, rocky, decorative. Woman unique, alive, essential. The artist quiet, without legs, an appendage of the drawing board. His flying characters, living in the heights, above the cornices.

The artist silhouetted by the table light, a metallic head with only one eye that's always watching what goes on in the belly of the board. Its characters bathed in moonlight.

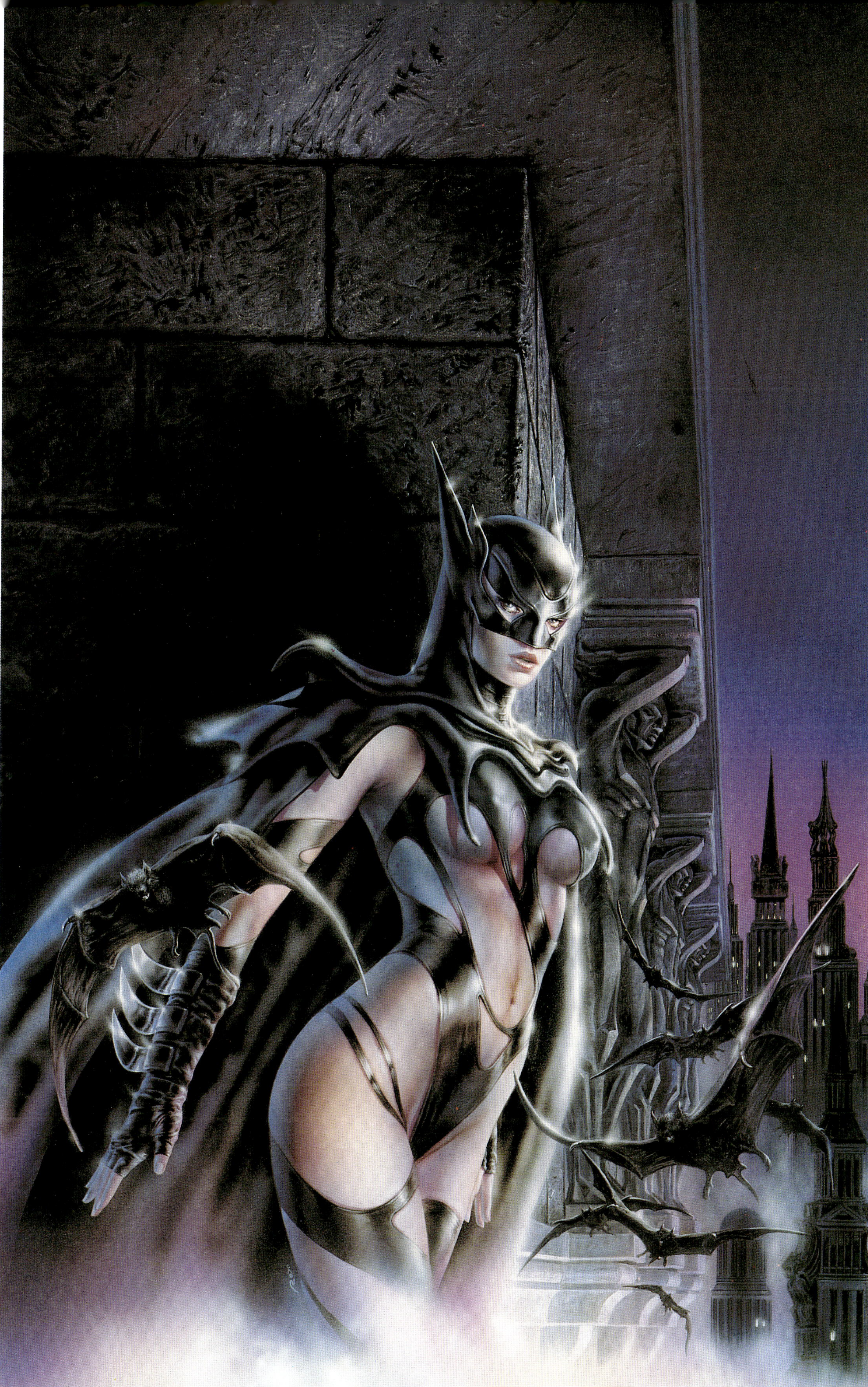

■ SHADOWRUN

1993

Dwarfs, elves, trolls and giants escape from the classic stories and invade the pavements of the future, leading us on to other adventures -- or perhaps to the same ones as always. They're the only ones who've ever moved us.

They can't be measured by the same scale as reality.

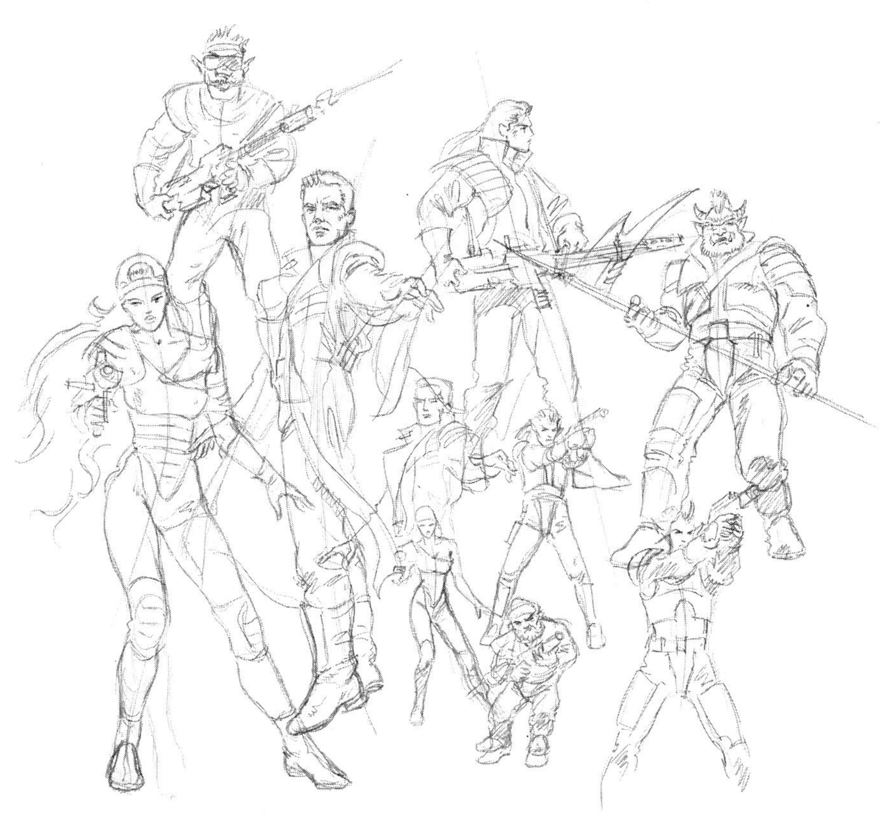

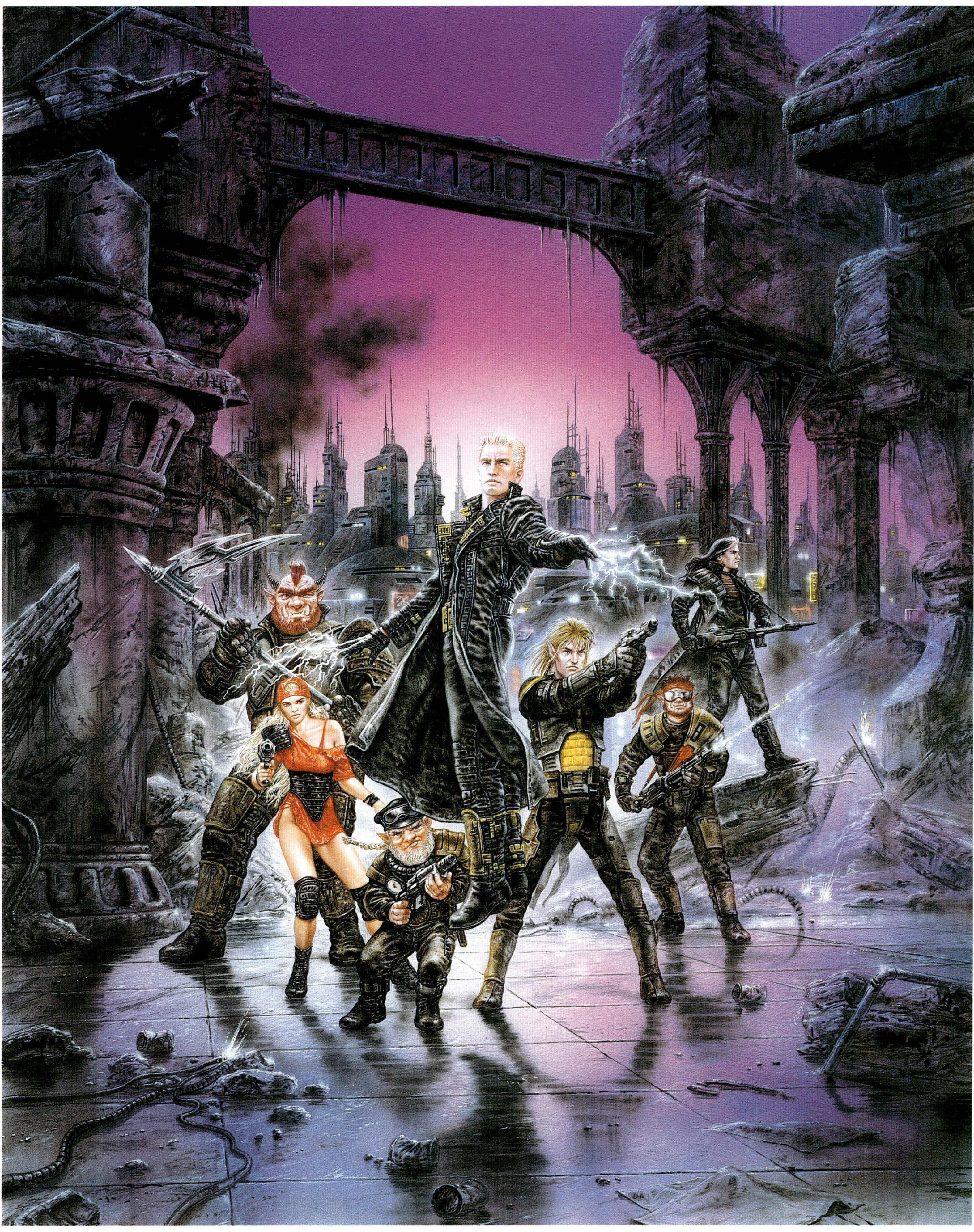

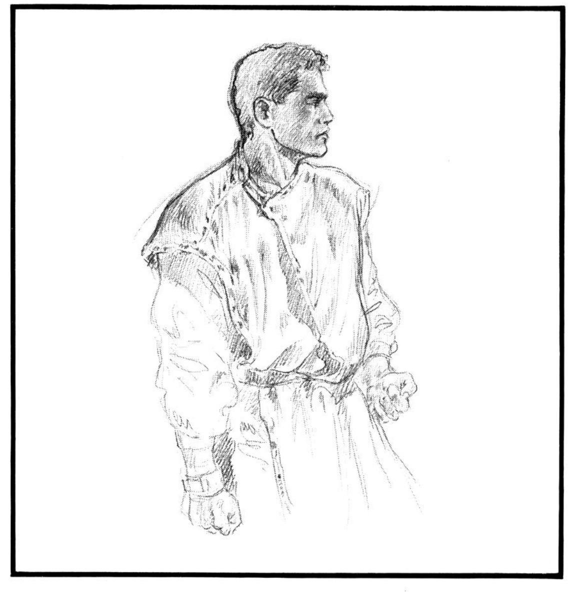

■ LEGEND OF THE DUELIST

1992

Instead of trying to show a future of immense majesty that bursts past the boundaries of the drawing, we can also show it in tiny, precious doses.

Instead of trying to show a big, challenging weapon, we can illustrate it with just a few sparkles.

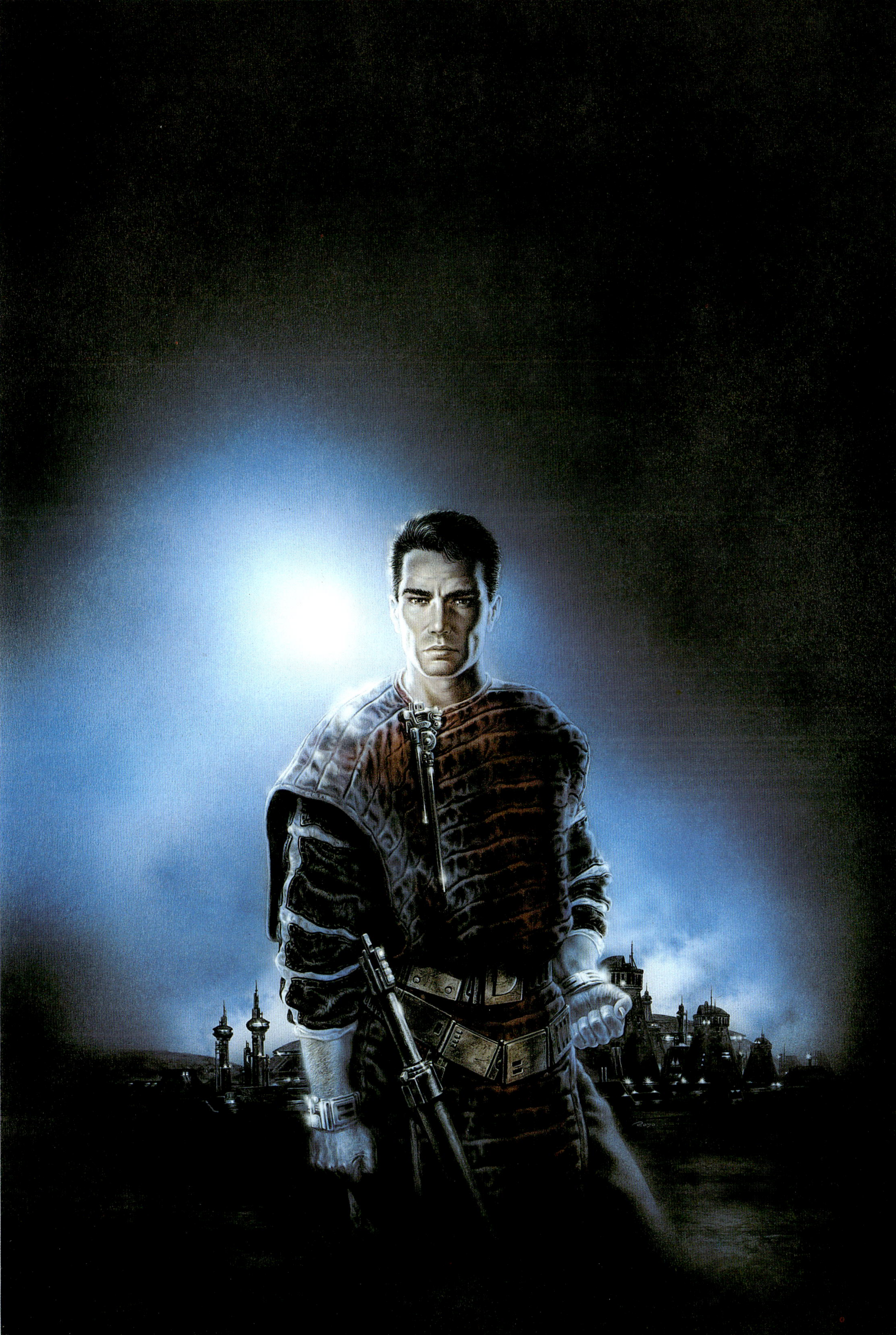

■ THE WHEELS OF TIME

1994

Rolling like the colors on a blank sheet of paper.
Between today and tomorrow. With no gestures that approach you.
With no place to sleep.

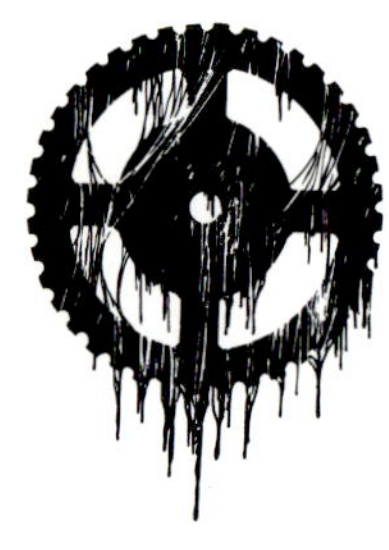

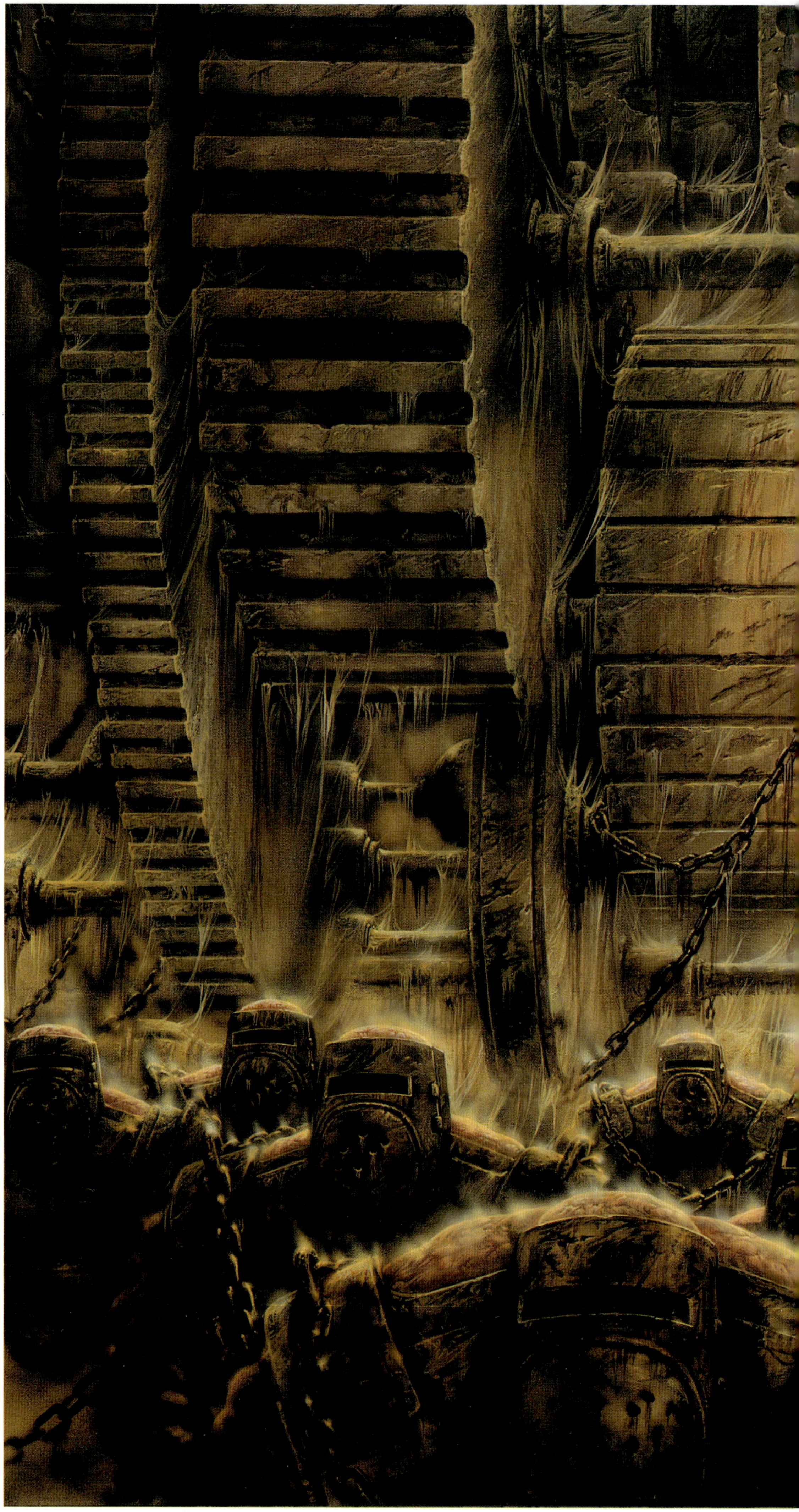

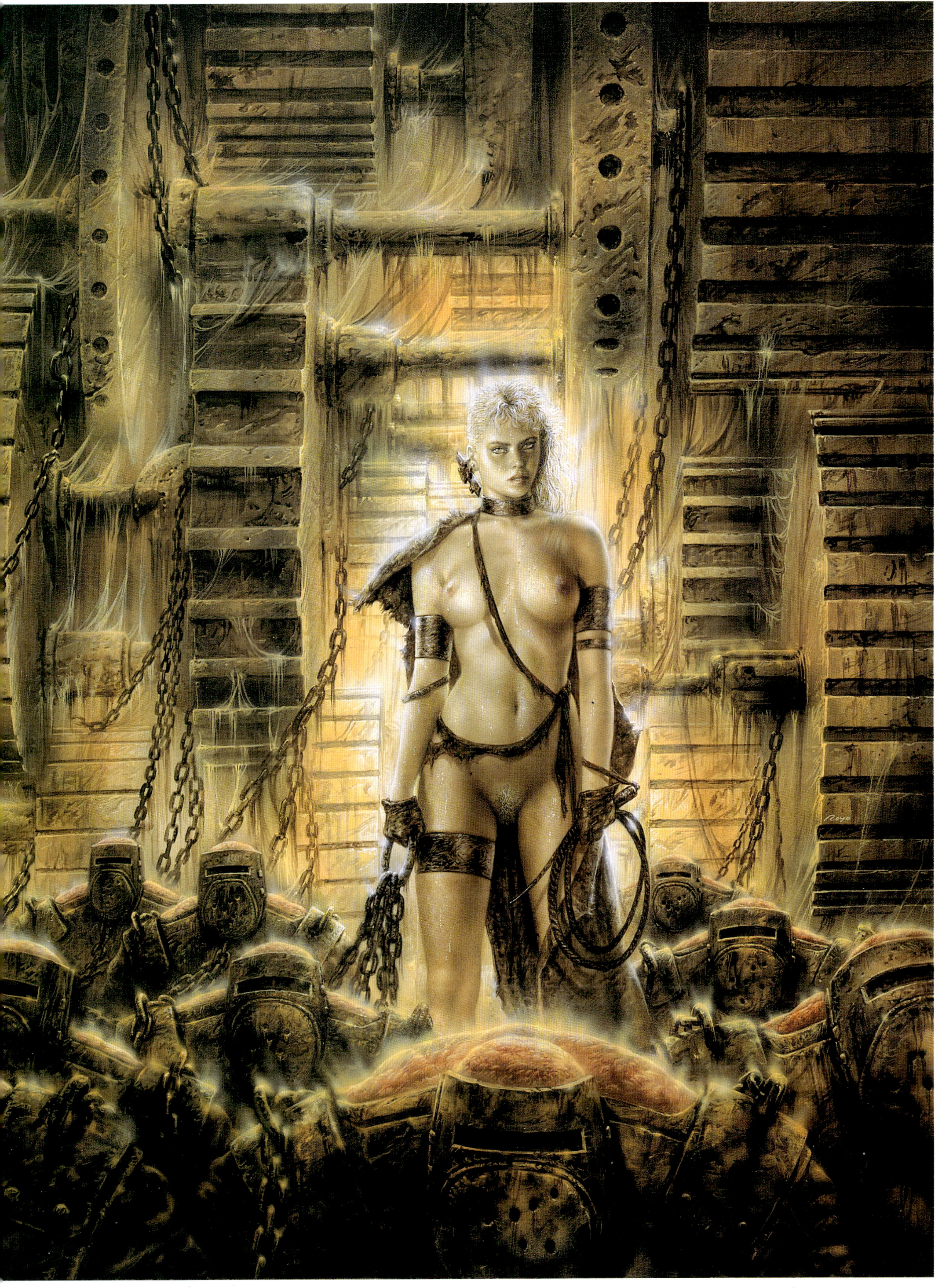
Royo

■ MALEFIC

1992

Behind any illustration there's only a trembling, insecure hand, and I believe that if that isn't so, it's not worth the trouble to look at. Behind a hand could be a look; behind the fingernails, a kiss. Behind desire is a beast.

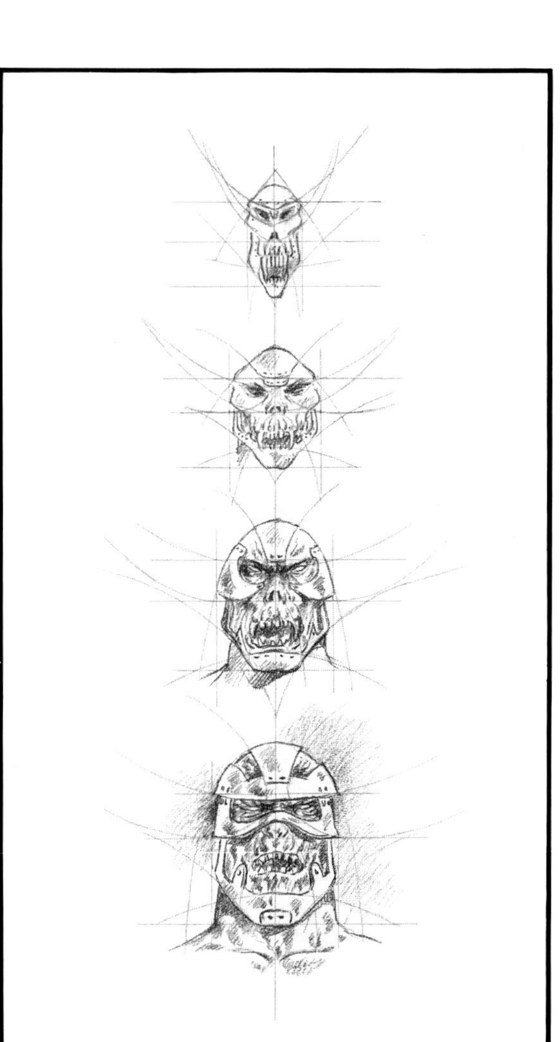

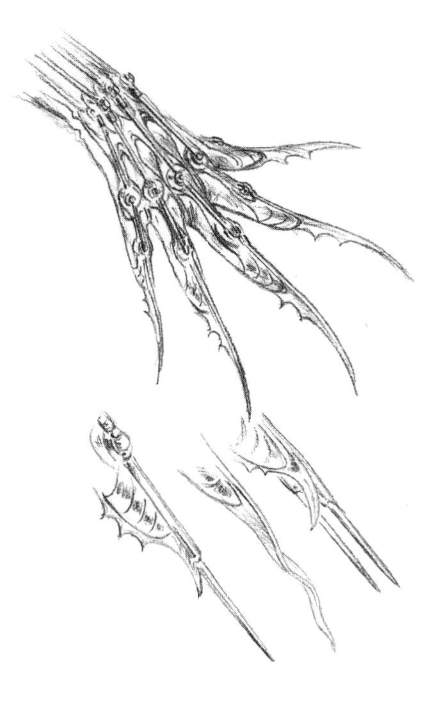

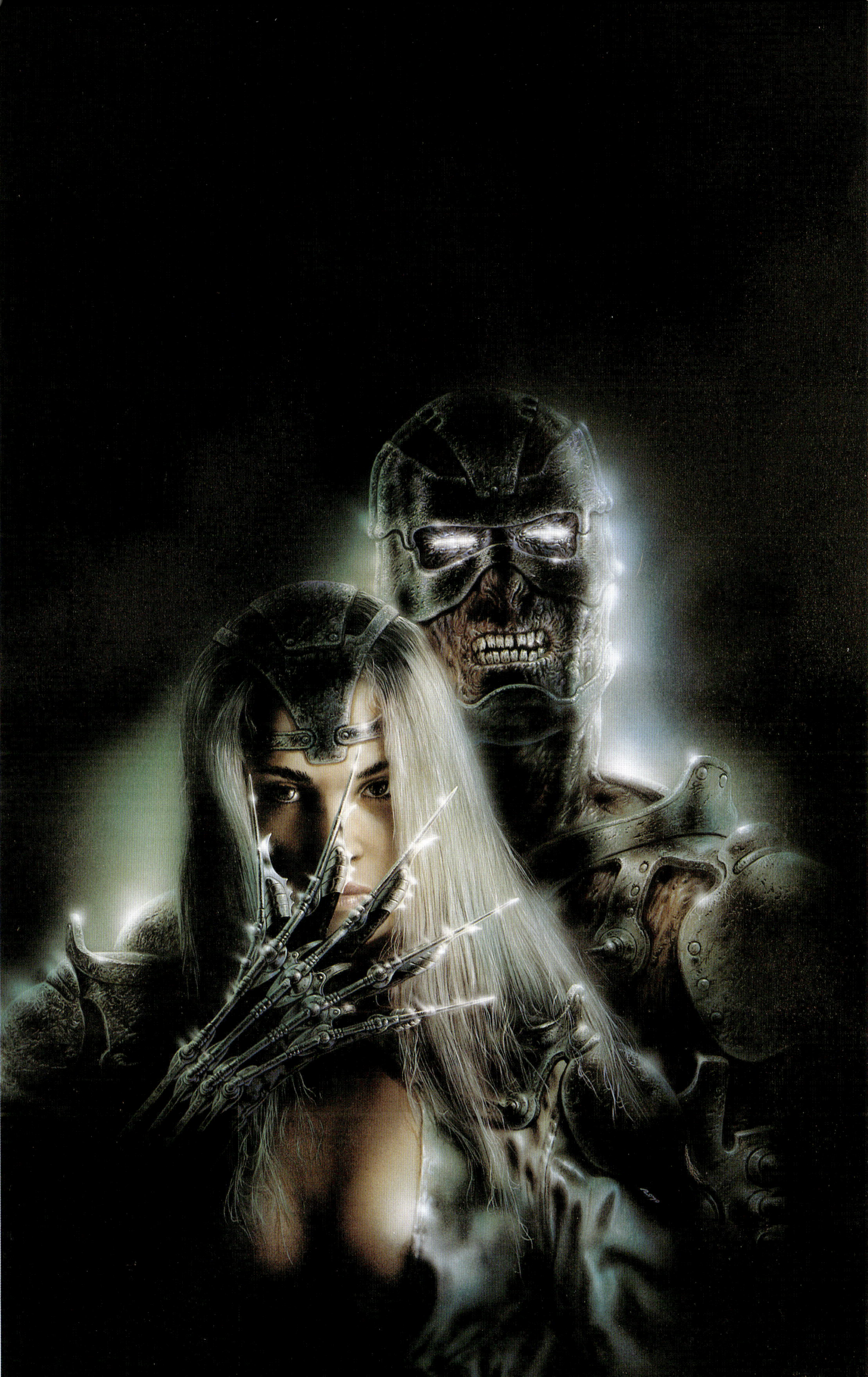

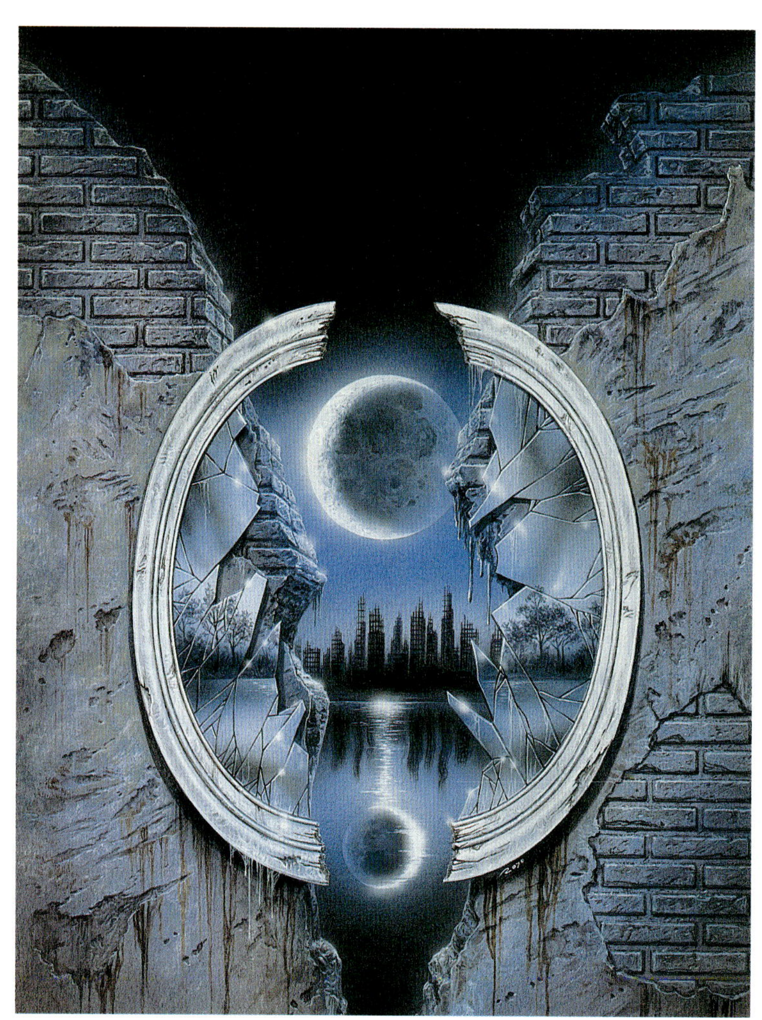

INDEX OF ILLUSTRATIONS

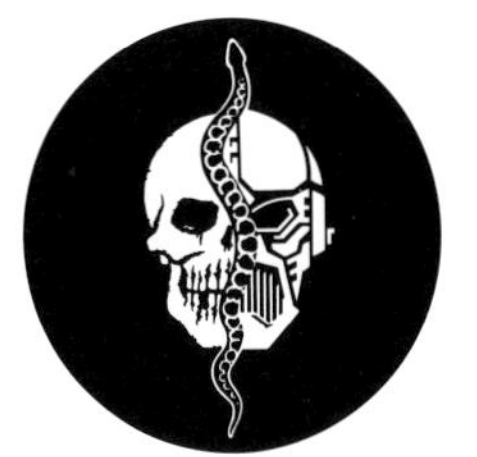